Scorched Earth Volume II

A Percentile RPG Story

Ethan Moore

Cover art by Kaitlyn Combs

This is a work of fiction. Names, characters, places, and incidents either are the product of the author's imagination or are used ficticiously. Any resemblance to actual person, living or dead, events, or locales is entirely coincidental.

ISBN: 978-1-968612-16-0

Printed in the U.S.A.

Contents

Chapter One
February 17th 2024
College Station, Texas
David Leibowitz

Another gutter ball.

David Leibowitz shrugged and walked back to the horse-shoe shaped couches where his roommate waited - bowling never had been his forte. His roommate's girlfriend had utterly shattered his heart the day before and for some reason, Collin thought he'd find the pieces in a bowling alley. So here they were.

It was 5:16pm on a Saturday and they were some of the only people in the business. City admin was still being strict on public restrictions due to the mysterious disease running roughshod through the former rebel states. David was surprised this place was open at all.

According to the CDC, the disease was allegedly a "shadow-borne illness" and caused hallucinations akin to night terrors while awake. As such, businesses were required to only operate during daylight hours and keep their premises as well-lit as possible.

A lot of people online were claiming the disease was released by the US government as retaliation for the rebel's actions in DC. Maybe it was a side effect of the nuclear exchange - David didn't know. He thought it was made up entirely but he couldn't conjure a reason as to why they'd do that.

Houston, Dallas, Austin, and Oklahoma City were still uninhabitable after ten years. DC had been hit by a chemical attack five years after the other cities were destroyed by nuclear bombs.

There was a company called Red Dunes trying to clean up the fallout using some new wonder technology they developed to terraform mars. He'd heard on the news that Red Dunes was planning on testing the terraforming tech this month in the affected cities. David had been a young kid when the war happened - he tried not to think about it often.

Collin was about as good at bowling as David, so they moved down to the arcade for a bit before getting an overpriced pizza to split. Collin talked about his girlfriend and David tried to listen, he really did, but he had a lot on his mind with school and the state of the world.

He was a student at A&M, working on a senior project he hoped could land him an internship with the Treighl Industries AI Applications branch. They were the designers of the guard robots that enforced the curfew laws on campus and around town. His duties mainly included overseeing maintenance of the units and making sure their diagnostic codes were reading appropriately.

He had, against protocol, kept a trashed trooper canine model that was going to get thrown out, and had been trying to repair it instead. He had also gotten into the crazy advanced programming itself and had begun trying to decode it - he found very little success but that was still a lot more than he had been expecting.

Last week Treighl Industries sent out an update to their "centaur" security bots to fix issues with communication distances and problem solving cognitives but it was causing more serious bugs in their behavior.

Treighl's lead designer must've been a nerd or something - all the model series' had fantasy names. Centaur, Dragon, Dullahan, Orc, Goblin, Kobalt, etc. The only exception he could think of was the Trooper line.

The head of the school's project, Dr. Harper, had alerted the company to the flaws they found but she wasn't ever able to get a response from the company. So she and David had taken it upon themselves to dig into it.

David realized the only thing he could hear was the cacophony of all the game's idle attraction noises - Collin had stopped talking and was staring at him.

"I'm sorry, man." David said, "I have a lot on my mind."

"I get it." Collin said, dejected and with a shrug.

An employee in a navy polo approached to tell them that the business would be closing in fifteen minutes due to curfew. They finished eating and headed back to their dorm.

Later that week, David strolled along, proud of what he'd done. The trooper model robot trotted alongside him - her segmented metal tail wagging happily with each step.

Dr. Harper had called him into the robotics lab - she thought she had figured out where the problem with the centaur bots was coming from and wanted them to start working on a fix. Two of the bots strode by them on the sidewalk. They had black and white plastic and gray silicone humanoid upper bodies suspended by a four-legged chassis that carried them - each had an energy rifle in their arms.

Their heads tracked David as they crossed paths - undoubtedly reading his ID badge he wore around his neck. He wondered how close the ones and zeros in those heads came to true thought.

One of his childhood friends was taking part in a project at a different university to transfer human brains into synthetic bodies. His friend had told him, in confidence, that they were having issues with synthetic brains they had made coping with the load of a human mind and that they were yet to successfully transplant anything.

David wondered what even happened to a person's soul in that situation - does it persist with the mind or does it reside somewhere else? If it resides with the mind, does making a copy of that also copy the soul? He shook the thoughts from his head before he got too far down that existential rabbit hole.

He walked into the well-lit and cold workspace that he shared with two other students and their lead professor.

Dr. Harper was sitting at a computer with her head in her hands. Amara+ coding blocks were etched across the monitor. She looked up when David got closer.

"Version two-fifteen did fix the comm errors - and the cognitive problems," she said, pointing to the blocks. "But I want you to look at this and tell me what you see."

David spent a few minutes looking at the code on the screen. A section labeled 'engagement permissions' was highlighted. It took him a while but he noticed the difference between 2.15 and 2.11. There was no check for oversight authorization to use lethal force against any individual. The term 'any individual' was also new. It used to utilize the phrase 'threat.'

"Wait, so what authorizes lethal force?"

"They do," she said, "each unit."

The thought of robots being the downfall of humanity, ala classic movies, had always been a topic that was joked about among the team when the robots first arrived. It didn't seem that funny anymore. The software editor program kicked David's login credentials. The professor tried and it kicked hers back too.

They spent the rest of the day trying to revert the software back to 2.11 or contact Treighl to let them know about the potentially deadly programming. Neither provided any results. Version 2.11 of the software had been deleted when the 2.15 update went through and Treighl was notorious for not responding to support calls. David could've sworn he'd made a backup of all the previous versions but the flash drives weren't in the labs.

Frustrated and tired, David called it a night and said goodbye to Dr. Harper - they'd have to keep working on this later. The trooper bot skipped along the sidewalk in front of him - turning around every once in a while to look back at him.

On their way back to his dorm, they were blocked on the sidewalk by a slender man in a black suit.

His swept back hair was so blond it looked almost white. His facial features were alarmingly gaunt and his cheekbones were the highest David had ever seen. His skin was milky white but David didn't think he looked pallid or off-putting - rather ethereal actually.

David tried to sidestep him on the pathway but the man held out a well-manicured hand to stop him.

"David Leibowitz?" he asked.

"Uh, yeah?" David replied, caught off guard.

"My name is Araless, I represent Treighl Industries." His voice carried a light lilting accent that David couldn't place. In fact, David was sure he had never heard an accent like it before.

"Good." David began, "I've been trying to get ahold of someone all day."

"We know." Araless said with a wry smile.

"Are your phones broken?" David was surprised to hear his brashness but he hadn't eaten since that morning and his work had grated on him. Araless would be the recipient of his just ire.

"No but there are things too sensitive to speak of on the phone." Araless squatted down to examine the trooper bot. He pulled out a small handheld device and held it up to the canine model. "It says here this unit was slated for decommission due to a complete failure on its axiom board. Why wasn't it turned in and destroyed?"

"I didn't feel right about throwing her in the dumpster. Soo, I took a crack at fixing her." David said, realizing now that he had probably broken all sorts of laws by cracking the robot's case.

"That is exceedingly impressive."

David was relieved to hear him say that.

"Thanks. Can I ask what you want, Mr. Araless?"

"Yes, you can." Araless said, nodding his head thoughtfully and standing back up. "I want - Treighl wants - to offer you a position. I'm even more sure of that decision now that I have seen this and I know they will agree," he said, motioning to the trooper bot.

David's mind raced at the possibility of working for Treighl Industries. It wasn't his goal when he applied for college but it had morphed into that during the last year of working on the robots. He'd be a fool to turn down this opportunity. Treighl had a finger in almost every industry on and off the planet - this could be a doorway into any job he could ever want. A gaggle of students passed them on the sidewalk. A patrol of centaur bots strolled by as well.

"Do your duty, stay inside," one of them said.

"Please have government ID's, as well as Vector ID's, available at all times," the other chimed in.

"Perhaps we can discuss this somewhere in private." Araless said, eying the students and ignoring the patrolling bots.

"Of course." David said, almost giggling at the thought of working for Treighl.

He led Araless back to his dorm room. Collin was out of town visiting his family in Kurten and wouldn't be back until the following day for classes. Out of town was a generous way to describe Kurten, but regardless, Collin wouldn't be there.

"I want to warn you, my dorm is a mess."

"I remember how scholam is." Araless said reassuringly.

David didn't question the odd terminology, his mind was still on his blindingly bright future.

They entered room 205 to a pile of Collin's dirty clothes that spanned the space between their twin beds. David made a general motion towards the clothes and shrugged at Araless. He sat down on the edge of his bed, facing the middle of the room, the trooper bot jumped onto the bed behind him.

"May I?" Araless asked, gesturing to David's desk chair.

David nodded and Araless stepped on the pile of clothes to get to the desk.

Had David been fully present, he may have noticed the clothes not depress fully under the weight of the full-grown man.

"About your employment," Araless began when he sat down. "It would have some strings attached. A vow of silence of course - excuse me - an NDA regarding anything you work on, see, hear, or experience by any other sense. We would also require you to keep secret anything you may have already seen while examining our products."

Something started to make sense in David's mind. Was he getting paid off to stay quiet about the issues they had found?

"We - I found something in the centaur's code that concerns me."

"I am aware." Araless said with the same wry smile. "Listen Mr. Leibowitz, the world is a dangerous place. There may come a time soon you will be thankful the Trustees are able to act in a way they see fitting."

"Have you ever read an Asimov book? You know, the three laws of robotics or anything like that? Has anyone at Treighl watched a movie?" David asked, again thinking about robots ushering in the end of humanity.

"This is the real world, David. You need to remember the real world has real dangers, real opportunities, and real consequences. Take the evening to think about it and call me in the morning with your answer." Araless stood and offered a metal business card with a phone number lightly embossed on the surface.

David laid awake in his dark dorm room as a thunderstorm raged in from the south. His heart raced and a knot had formed solidly in the pit of his stomach. He tried to pray for an answer but he couldn't summon the words. He slipped his phone off the nightstand and looked at the time after. *1 AM.* He thumbed through his contacts until he came to Lance Conway. Lance was David's friend from childhood who was studying brain to computer interfacing. Lance's family had practically raised David. He opened the contact and started typing.

"Hey Lance, I need to talk to you about something. I know it's late but can we meet halfway. It's really important."

They had been friends since elementary school during the short secession war and made a point to hangout when they could now that they were both in college - Lance went to school about an hour and a half north. They'd occasionally meet at a 24-hour fast-food place on the highway in Calvert. The restaurant would be closed right now due to the curfew restrictions but they could still meet in the parking lot. His phone buzzed with Lance's reply.

"I'll bring a shovel."

The world was so peaceful at this hour - the Trustee Bots made sure of it. As it was, he had to sneak out of his dorm and evade their patrols to get here.

David looked around the dimly lit parking lot outside of a closed diner. The only sounds came from his engine idling and the trooper bot in the back seat adjusting her position every few minutes. He hadn't seen a single car on the way up here. If he had to make a call right now, he'd say he was the only human in the county.

Gravel crunched outside as a car parked in the spot next to him. The passenger door of David's car shut as Lance settled into the seat. David laughed when he saw the shovel in Lance's car.

"I woke my dad up getting that from their garage. He was pissed - worth it. What's up, man?" Lance asked through a yawn.

"Treighl offered me a job."

"That's great! But why didn't you just put that in a text?"

"I found some lethal bugs in their software and I'm pretty sure they're hiring me to keep my mouth shut about it. Well, I thought they were bugs but apparently, they're intentional."

"Like, 'it's not a bug, it's a feature?' kinda thing?" Lance asked.

"No. I think it's more like a 'Bond villain, secret kill switch for society type thing.' 'Press the big red button and all the robot's eyes go from blue to red' kind of thing." David said, leaning back into his seat.

"That's, uh, that's big."

"Yeah. And the guy that approached me - he was this weird cross between a man in black and the slenderman."

"G-man."

"Yeah, similar vibe but less monotone, I guess? I don't know what to do. I could join them and try to change things from inside. Or, I could refuse and he'll probably kill me."

"Aw buddy, and you've brought me into this? And it's deadly? Who needs enemies…"

David had already emailed Lance about the update issues but that was before Treighl had gotten directly involved. He probably shouldn't have done that on their school accounts. It was too late now.

The storm caught up to them in Calvert. Rain started beating on the roof of his car.

"I don't think I'll be able to work for them." David said, watching the trails of rain on his windshield.

"Well, David, I want you to know that you've always been my best friend and knowing you has meant the world to me."

David laughed with his friend but he didn't argue with the implication.

The trooper yipped from the back seat. Its back vents were raised like hackles - its attention was on the building's lobby.

There was someone inside. At least it looked like there had been for a second but the figure vanished into a wisp of black smoke that blew away in the dining room of the dingy restaurant. Lance swore bitterly under his breath.

"I wish we were burying a body instead," he said.

"Did you see that too?" David asked.

"I thought maybe I was sick."

They parted ways shortly after they saw the figure. David didn't get back to his dorm room until after four in the morning. There was a folded note slipped under his door.

"David, I came by to discuss the update roll back but you weren't answering the door. I don't trust email

or phone right now. Meet me at Evans 324 first thing in the morning. 7:30 AM.
I remembered what happened to the backup drives. You took them to work on the dog.
-Evelyn"

He collapsed on his bed, blinked, and was wrenched from sleep by his 7:00 AM alarm. He grabbed the backup drive from his desk and dropped it into his pocket. Then he grabbed his satchel, stumbled into the hall, locked the door, and made his way to the library to meet Dr. Harper.

He had been in these study rooms before. They were small with a conference table and usually a window that looked out into the hall. Probably more so the window looked into the room to make sure students weren't doing anything untoward.

He passed a Treighl Industries Trustee Bot, as the centaur bots had been marketed to the school system. They were supposed to be the safer alternative to human police - less volatile, less prone to bad judgement calls. He opened the door into the study room. His heart fell out of his chest.

Dr. Harper was sitting slack in a chair opposite the door - blood darkened the maroon sweatshirt she was wearing and her face was devoid of expression. The wall behind her had several scorched bullet holes - the central ones were surrounded in her blood.

Araless sat in a chair across from her, he was turned to face David. He casually held a strange looking pistol aimed at him. He stood. David's heart was pounding. He lunged at the strange man and rammed into his body. It gave way much easier than David had expected.

Shots were fired from the pistol and it was knocked to the ground. David grabbed it and shakily aimed it at Araless. The man was nowhere to be seen - just a wisp of black smoke hung in the air.

The centaur bot he had seen earlier rounded the corner into view of the doorway. David slammed the door shut but the robot started trying to beat it down. He hoisted the table in the way to block the entry.

"Everyone remain calm, there appears to be an active shooter on campus," the bot said.

It seemed clear to David that he was well and truly screwed. Even if he made it out of here without getting killed by Araless, he'd get buried for murdering his professor.

"In for a penny I guess," he muttered to himself. At least he could disable the centaur bots and have done some good maybe.

He aimed Araless' pistol at the door and squeezed off a handful of blasts. The gun let out a high-pitched squeal indicative of an energy weapon. The robot outside stopped talking as it fell heavily to the ground. David tried to open the door but he wasn't able to. He grabbed a chair and broke the large window.

David heard screaming coming from other parts of the library. He climbed through the broken window and grimaced as the glass cut his arm. His satchel fell as he climbed through. He landed on the other side harder than he should have. Pain coursed through his body from his midsection. He reached down and found blood seeping from his stomach.

Welp - none of this was going to be his problem for very much longer.

He pulled himself up and stumbled down the hallway. He got his phone to call Lance and tell him what was happening - just so someone would know the truth.

The phone went to voicemail. He chuckled ruefully and put the phone back in his pocket. Almost his entire family had been killed in the nuclear blasts that leveled Houston ten years ago. The ones who had survived died later from the radiation. Lance was the only person he had to call.

Outside, students were running for buildings - nobody was concerned with him. He made his way to the control room on top of the academic center.

He was in the middle of the courtyard when he felt something sharp bite across his throat. Blood began pouring out. He spun around to see Araless standing with an ornate knife in his hand. That same creepy smile was on his face.

Araless opened his mouth to speak but was cut off. His head was turned into a mass of meat and bone by his own gun. Blood and brain matter sprayed on the campus sidewalk.

David dropped the weapon and clutched his throat to hold the bleeding.

Araless' body crumpled onto the concrete now having remised its connection to life. David knew he only had a few minutes left before he met his end as well.

"Firestorm inbound. ETA fifteen minutes," one of the Trustee Bots said.

David didn't know what the hell that meant. He quickly made his way up the stairs to the utility room where the ladder to the roof was. He heard a yip behind him as he moved through the building.

He was alarmed to see how much blood he had left behind. The trooper bot raced up to him - an expression of concern was on her face. Together they got to the ladder. David tried to climb it but the strength had drained from his body and his hands were slick with his blood. A Trustee Bot in the hallway made another call. Five minutes until firestorms. It advised seeking shelter.

He tried a couple times to climb the ladder but eventually gave up and fell to the ground. He curled up next to the whimpering trooper bot, gurgling a few words of encouragement to his metal companion. David Liebowitz took in a ragged breath and closed his eyes for the last time.

Minutes later, rebounding waves of fire engulfed the globe. Scorched and dead, the world moved on.

Chapter Two
October 14th, 2114
Ferrell Building, Waco Texas
Gertrude Alvarez

"Gertrude, you have realized the Oracle's will. Look happy about it," the robed council member said as the Trustee Bots continued running boot diagnostics. Gerti had a tightness in her chest - she could barely breathe.

"I don't understand." Gerti felt dazed.

The members of the research order buzzed around the room checking different monitors for status' and unit diagnostics. Gerti was nauseated.

"The Oracle said the reviving scripts would be at the other university. I'm ashamed to say, I thought I wouldn't live to see the awakening of the Oracle's holy army," the councilman said. "We can finally sanctify these lands and rule like we've been trying to do for all these years. The mutants, the Bell family, the monsters… the damn rebels. None of them will be a problem for us anymore and we have you to thank for that. I'm sure that's reward enough but the crystal will be delivered to your family's home. I know I'm getting ahead of myself, since you're not officially initiated yet, but my name is Hector Emberlain. I want you to think of me as a friend now. You've done all of us a great service." He shook her hand. All thoughts in Gerti's head about firm handshakes went out the window as she stared at the unlimbering robots.

Gerti thought about smashing the computers in the room and killing everyone she could before the guards could take her out. She had no idea she would be giving them this much power by completing their job. She realized the rebels were gonna have to fight these bots now. Fresh bots. Not the dilapidated and ragged things she had fought and almost died to. The creeping things that had terrorized the Brazos valley for nearly a century.

She started to breathe rapidly as her heart rate picked up. Her tongue stuck to the roof of her mouth.

"Can I go?" she managed to ask.

"Of course, Gertrude. Come by the Council before too long. I want to take you to the Oracle so you can take your oath to be a bear - in earnest now." Councilman Emberlain said.

Gerti stepped out into the harsh sunlight and walked through the shanty town that surrounded the inner district. She arrived at her father's clinic.

It used to be a student housing building that had been used as part of the inner wall when it was constructed. It was one of the only buildings in the outer section that was frequented by the council members and the citizens of the inner circle. The Council had tried to pay her father to move his clinic into the inner walls but he had held out knowing that outer citizens wouldn't be able to utilize his services anymore.

The smell of mildew was everywhere in these old buildings - to the point where it was a wholly nostalgic smell to her. Gwen was waiting inside the old living room turned waiting room. They were the only two in the clinic's lobby.

"Hey, how'd it go?" Gwen asked.

"I think I really messed up." Gerti sat down on a couch and let the cushions absorb her. "The drive was to run Trustee Bots. They want to use them to fight the rebels."

"Rebels?" Gwen asked.

The rebels had been using the clinic for years. Her father had managed to keep it a secret from the Council. Many of Gerti's friends growing up had become rebels, and a lot of them had been killed by council guards, bears, or the wilds.

"People who think the Council're tyrants."

"Are they right?" Gwen asked.

"I mean, I see where they're coming from. A lot of people out here don't like being told what to do."

"The world's pretty wide. Why don't they leave?"

"They have. Any time someone leaves to start a new settlement it gets taken out overnight. The rebels think it's the Council forcing a point. The Council always says it's just the wasteland doing what the wasteland does best. I don't know what to do here, Gwen." Gerti sank into the couch cushions.

"What do you mean?"

"They want me to become a bear."

"I thought you already were one."

"Not yet, not completely." Gerti said, shaking her head. "I would need to take an oath to their Oracle and renounce any other faith I have."

"Oh wow. That's intense." Gwen said.

A slender specter of a woman cast a long shadow through the front entry. She was a severe looking woman who had seen this horrible world and survived some of the worst it could throw at her and it showed clearly. Gerti shot up and gave her mom a hug.

"Gropht told me you were back," the woman said.

Gerti began to cry into her mother's shoulder. She hadn't realized how much the past month had weighed on her. The three of them sat down around a small table in the kitchen so that they could recount the events of Gertrude's journey to her mother.

Finally, Gerti told her about the Trustee Bots in the Ferrell building and what they were capable of.

"What should I do, Mom?"

"Join them." her mom said definitively.

"But we're -" Gerti began.

"Get in there and kill the Oracle. Anybody who's tried before was sniffed out or killed before any damage could be done. This is our chance to cripple the Council."

Gerti was taken aback by her mother's sudden cold fervor.

"You want me to swear an oath to the Oracle? You'd always tell me the story of Daniel going into Bab -"

"They ration our food, drive us into the wilderness on their behalf, and kill us whenever we've tried to do anything about it. They steal children, they imprison and execute alleged rebels with no evidence. They almost executed you. Gertrude, this isn't Babylon. And Daniel didn't have to fight computer driven death robots. God will understand."

Gerti's parents had always raised her to stand by her values no matter what was going on. She had never heard her mother say anything so directly against her upbringing like this - it hit her like a brick. As far as Daniel and his friends were concerned, Gerti thought they had to face a lot worse than these robots. She nodded her head thoughtfully for a silent few moments of shock before she stood up from the table.

"Gwen, I need some air - I'm gonna go for a walk. D'you wanna see the town?"

Gwen nodded and followed her out the front door of the clinic. They walked towards the outer wall back to the market where they had entered earlier that morning.

"You okay?" Gwen asked.

"Hell no. My mom's tellin' me to forsake my God so I can have a chance to kill the Council's leader. It's crazy."

"She seems to think it'll be okay."

"You don't understand Gwen - I can't. It's not going to happen. I'll find somethin' else to deal with this."

"What if you just go talk to the Oracle? Just to get more info." Gwen asked.

"Hm. Maybe."

"Moonbeam!" a man called out to them.

He was a slightly rotund Hispanic man in his forties carrying a carpet bag in one hand and a plastic sack in the other. Both were filled with medical supplies. Her dad ran and gave her a hug - tears streamed down his cheeks.

"I knew you'd make it back. I knew you would," he said. "If anyone could make that trip, it was going to be you or your mother."

They laughed together.

Her mother Elena was mythic among the community as unkillable. Many things had tried, few had stood a chance, and even fewer had come close. Other badlanders called her Elena 'Razorback' Alvarez for killing the legendary king of the mutated hogs in her early days.

"Oh Dad, this is my friend Gwen. We met on my trip. She helped me a lot."

"To be fair, I think I still owe you one." Gwen said.

"I guess it depends on how you count it." Gerti replied.

"I got shot in the leg. Gerti got a tourniquet on me and bandaged it. I probably would've bled out." Gwen said.

"She's learned a lot from her mom but she got that one from me," he said, beaming at his daughter. "It's nice to meet you, Gwen. Thanks for being there for my baby girl."

Gerti relayed her situation with the Council and what her mother had said to her dad. He closed his eyes and listened intently to the story.

"Your mother's been through a lot with the Council," he said. "You have to forgive her. We've lost a lot of close friends to them - your uncle when he left…"

"But to ask me to - I don't know Dad."

"Just be careful with them. I thought I might never see you again and I don't want to risk losing you because of your mom's vendetta." He shook his head and smiled.

"I know you're going to do the right thing. I'm so happy you're back but I'm exhausted and hungry. I'll set up a cot for your friend. Come back when you can - I want to hear about your trip."

They hugged again and he took off towards the clinic. Gerti and Gwen were left alone in the little side street.

"Okay. I'll talk to the Oracle - just to get more information." Gerti said.

"If they're so bad, why'd you work for them in the first place?" Gwen asked.

"It was easy crystal at first. I was basically already doing the job so I figured I'd get paid by them."

"What were you doing?"

"There's a list of mundane pre-fire items they will pay for - so I'd find those in old houses around town and bring them back. I'd patrol our neighborhood, occasionally guard the clinic, and sometimes I'd go hunting with my mother. They arrested me after I refused to kill Mr. Gropht. I think they thought I was a rebel."

"Is that why you were looking for the drive?" Gwen asked.

Gerti nodded.

"They arrested me and told me I needed to prove my loyalty. I could either go to College Station, or get executed. Now I think they were hopin' I'd just die out there so they didn't have to worry about if I was a rebel or not," she said.

They walked together to the entrance of the building leading to the council chamber. The two guards standing in front of it stopped them. They were wearing shimmering silver plate armor that had been trimmed with gold and they carried spears with tips that danced in the sunlight.

Everyone in the inner wall looked too clean for Gerti's liking and they were all wearing robes of solid colors. A lot of them were wearing jewelry that caught the light in ethereal shimmers like the guard's armor.

The guards made the sign of the bear, a hand held up mimicking a bear claw, and opened the doors for her and Gerti and led them to the council chamber.

Inside, Hector Emberlain was one of only a few council members present. His face lit up when he saw Gerti.

"I wanna meet the Oracle before I swear an oath. I think that's only fair." Gerti said.

"You don't even meet the Oracle during the oath. Most inner citizens aren't even allowed to meet them," he said, his face suddenly flushed.

"If I'm going to renounce my faith and swear allegiance to a mysterious entity, I'd at least like to meet it first."

"That's just not an option. I'm sorry," he said.

"Hey, has anybody else done more for the Council than her?" Gwen asked, gesturing to Gerti.

It was a genuine question and Gerti was betting that nobody had. Emberlain furrowed his brow and thought for a moment before replying.

"I suppose not," he finally said.

He motioned for them to follow him. Inner wall citizens watched them disdainfully as they walked by. Guard's eyes followed them. He led the girls through the buildings on the old campus, alongside a large ditch that dropped off to their right, up to a U-shaped brick building with large windows. Large white letters labeled the structure as *"Marrs Science Building."*

"It's amazing to see how this place has persisted through the fires." Emberlain said pensively.

"What do you mean?" Gwen asked.

"This used to be one of the nation's highest institutions of learning - senators and captains of business graduated from these halls. Now that we have our army, scholars for thousands of years will trace civilization's return to this day and this place. I will personally ensure that those histories will have the name 'Gertrude Alvarez' in bold."

They entered the old science building. The inside wasn't like the other campus. This one had been cleaned out and damage had been repaired with care. They went down hallways until they came to a section labeled ESAP. Underneath the letters, the acronym was elongated - Elysian Synaptic Ascension Project.

They entered the double doors to reveal more hallways with metal doors lining the walls. Ornate school banners had been hung from the laboratory walls and ceiling. A foul smell hit them. Two council bears carried buckets of refuse past them and apologized to the council member as they went through the double doors. Emberlain smiled at Gerti.

"The Oracle is in the room at the far end of the hall, with the guard. I'll take you. Would your friend mind waiting out here?" he said, side-eying Gwen.

"You gonna be alright?" Gwen asked.

* * *

Gerti nodded and turned to follow Emberlain into the room at the end of the hall. He closed the door behind them.

The girl sat down on a plastic bench that had been placed between two closed doors. She leaned her head against the wall and closed her eyes - the road coming up here had worn her out and she needed the rest.

Someone was crying - it sounded like the room behind her. She could barely hear it. She looked around - the Oracle's guard had gone into the chamber with the councilman and Gerti. She stood up and put her ear to the door closest her and listened for the sorrowful sounds.

It was there but it was faint. She twisted the knob and was surprised to find it was unlocked.

Inside the room was an arrangement of old computer monitors and lab equipment. A thick layer of dust covered every surface. The fires hadn't touched this room it seemed.

In the center of the wall opposite the door were three tanks. They were about three feet wide circular structures with windowed doors. The two on either side were closed but the one in the middle was open, revealing a padded chair with armrests. Sitting in the chair were the mummified remains of a person. The corpse's clothes were torn by a large gash across the torso - slight remnants of discoloration surrounded the tear. The figure had a metal crown resting on its head that was attached to the tank by a large harness of thick cables. She heard the crying again.

"Please help me. Somebody... Anybody," a young man's voice muttered through bouts of crying - tired and defeated.

The lips weren't moving and no breath was expelled but the girl knew the voice was coming from the corpse.

* * *

Gerti entered the room in front of Emberlain. It was an old laboratory filled with darkened computer monitors. Banners hung from the ceiling here like in the hallway. A small arrangement of fragranced candles were lit on a small table near the far end of the room. A single circular metallic chamber leaned against the wall in a mounting array.

A mass of black fur sat in a chair centered in the chamber. A metallic skullcap hung from the ceiling, suspended by a jumbled mass of cords, and rested on the head of a withering, wheezing bear carcass. The fur of the bear had worn off in sections and it was severely emaciated - its exposed skin was covered in lesions that left marred craters that bubbled with pustules. White foam collected around the corners of its mouth. Yellowed teeth protruded past its thin jowls. It looked like a miserable creature to Gerti - was this the Oracle? There was no way on God's burned Earth she was going to swear any kind of anything to this creature.

"Gertrude, this Judge Legio - the Oracle." Emberlain said, as he bowed towards the mutated bear and made a reverent claw salute with his right hand.

It worked its jaw to open its diseased mouth as if to speak. Its voice came from speakers in the corners of the small room - static of the dying devices made it difficult for Gerti to hear clearly. She strained to make out the words.

"Getrude Alvarez. Daughter of Elena the great hunter, and our esteemed doctor Luis," it began. Its voice was a choir of countless other voices, men and women, joined to be one entity. "We have seen that you have performed a miracle for us by reviving the long dead robots on our campus. For completing your task faithfully, you are being granted the honor of meeting us in addition to the position as a bear. To continue serving us until the last of your days. Swear your allegiance to the Council, and to us, so we can begin with the rest of your task."

The overlaid voices sent a cold shiver up Gerti's spine into the base of her skull.

"Hold on. I have some questions first," she said.

The bear's tilted head coughed abruptly in a way that sounded like a scoff to Gerti. The speakers remained silent, save for the unnerving buzz, so Gertrude continued.

"What are you?" she asked.

"We are the Oracle. We have observed this world for untold years. We have watched over our wards and kept the evils of this world at bay since before the fires that consumed our world."

"That's what you do - not what you are."

"Gertrude." Emberlain began to interject but he was cut off with a grimacing laughter from the speakers.

"You think we are a monster? Or perhaps a demon. Which is it, Child?" the speakers hissed and popped.

"Whichever hat's got your name on it." Gerti said, putting her hands in her pockets.

"I did not bring you here to insult the Oracle!" Emberlain yelled.

"Silence! You do not exist to defend me against girls. In that, I am more than capable," the Oracle boomed. Gerti thought she'd be able to take this bear carcass in a one on one if it came to that. It already looked seven eighths dead anyways. One of the speakers popped and fizzled out. Everyone in the room flinched.

"Emberlain, I believe one of our priests requires your attention in the hallway."

Emberlain nodded and quickly left the room.

The bear waited a moment before shifting its milky eyes back towards Gerti.

"We are neither a monster nor a demon. Our essence exists in the void between the realms of the living and the dead. It has granted us powers beyond your comprehension and opened our eyes to the truth of god and the afterlife - but it has also trapped us here. Partitioned from life - withheld from the release of death. We've acted upon the mortal world through the Council but the time has come for us to claim new bodies and preside over our charge. If you continue to help us, as you already have, you will have a position in our grand world."

"Let's say I agree. What would I be doing?"

"After you swear your oath to us, you will be helping the council to eradicate or convert the remaining rebels. You will be saving their lives by convincing them that continuing to fight would be a useless endeavor. We need as many of them alive as possible if we're going to survive."

"What happens to the rebels who resist?"

"Their foolishness cannot be allowed to persist. They will be given an opportunity to join the right side. So, will you help us bring a new age of light to this dark world?"

Gerti wanted to reply with a simple 'no' but she didn't want to anger the abomination in front of her. The thought of working for this demonic creature who had probably ordered so many awful things was unthinkable. She wanted to ask what had happened to the outer citizens that had left or where people went when they disappeared but she felt she had pushed her luck enough as it was.

"I need a little time to consider it," she said finally.

"You do not have very much time to make your decision. Our plans will proceed with or without you."

"I understand."

The doors to the chamber opened quietly as Emberlain came in again.

"Pardon, Priest Aytarun just informed me that the Trustee B - your metal vessels will take some time to get running." Emberlain said.

"Two weeks. We were privy to your conversation." The Oracle's voice wheezed through the speakers. Gerti hadn't heard any of it but she presumed the Oracle was referring to "themselves" instead of it and her.

"That is your time, Child. You have until our bodies are ready."

* * *

The girl bent down beside the desiccated corpse and listened for the cries again. She realized it wasn't coming from the corpse itself but a little thin black rectangle in its lap. She gingerly picked it up and wiped the dust off the surface. She saw her reflection in the black mirror.

There was a wisp of a face behind her. It was a young man with soft features, brown hair, and tear-stained cheeks. She turned around to see there was nobody behind her.

"Please help me - whoever you are. I've been alone for so long," a voice said.

The girl could see the person's mouth moving a second before she heard his voice coming out the end of the black mirror in her hand.

Chapter Three
October 14th, 2114
Alvarez Clinic, Waco Texas
Elena Alvarez

Elena Alvarez silently scaled the outside of the clinic towards the roof. Once she reached the top she sat on the edge and watched the sunset in the distance. She tried to remember her parent's faces but she couldn't. It had been dark and Elena was very young when it happened - none of the details were ever clear in her mind's eye. In later years, her older brother Caleb or her own rationalizations would fill in a lot of gaps.

Her parents had taken her and Caleb out into the wasteland to start a new life away from the Council. They settled in the metal shells of an old business center along one of the highways. She was too far removed from the events to remember exactly where it had been.

Raiders had attacked at night and wiped out all the adults. She remembered that much. There had been no conversation and no mercy - it was a one-sided slaughter. Once the raiders had finished killing the adults, they left. She and her brother had been the only survivors. The Council's Bears found them a week later and brought them back to Waco.

She was an adult before she saw the pattern with other separatist settlements but that hadn't been enough to make her join the rebels. There just wasn't enough concrete evidence for her. Out of gratitude, Caleb had worked hard to become a Bear so he could go out and save people like they had saved him. He got what he wanted when he was sixteen.

Elena was thirteen when she felt her brother slipping away. The Council took him into their chambers so he could sell his soul to them and their Oracle. Her brother's personality changed when he took his oath. He became a fanatical supporter of the Council and wouldn't shut up about how wise the Oracle was.

It felt like she lost part of her brother. He talked about their leader like he was an infallible god. It was sickening but she put up with it because she loved him and she didn't want to push away the only family she had.

One day he was given a project by the Council and he never came back. It was that simple and that quick. Not even that made her join the rebels. Elena lost her fear in the years following Caleb's disappearance. There wasn't a situation dangerous enough for her to turn her back on.

Truthfully, she had tried to die but nothing would do the trick. She had run into storms of gunfire without being touched - fought a hog that weighed two tons with a knife and had managed to kill it. It gave her a reputation throughout Waco as an unkillable legend.

By the time she met Luis and they had Gertrude, the evils of the Council were clearly apparent but they had seemed manageable. They'd leave you alone if you played by their rules and stayed in line. She hadn't heard about Gertrude being arrested until they had already sent her away on their project. Dozens of bears had been sent before her and none of them ever made it back.

When she heard that Gertrude had been sent away, Luis had to physically restrain her from killing every council member she could get her hands on. It had been a struggle for him. In that moment, she would have ripped out the spines of everybody in the town if it meant Gertrude being safe.

Once she had been able to get a breath in her lungs, she made a bee-line for Bezral Gropht to help the rebels. Everyone suspected he was involved with them. He was too old to be a fighter but she knew a lot of the younger citizens looked up to him as the paragon of defiance against the Council. Within hours she was meeting with organizers. They were ecstatic to finally have the unkillable Elena Alvarez on their side. She had felt herself slipping back into the fearless Elena she had known before Gertrude.

It was difficult for her to accept that maybe the status quo could return now that Gertrude was back. She didn't think she could pretend the Council didn't need to be routed. It's not like she had a choice on how things went right now anyway. As she sat here, her daughter was negotiating with the devil for her soul.

She knew Gertrude would do the right thing and listen to her mother.

* * *

Gerti stepped out of the Oracle's chamber into the lab hallway. Gwen was nowhere to be seen.

"Where's your friend?" Emberlain asked.

"How the hell should I know?" Gerti replied. "Gwen?" she called out.

Gwen responded with a muffled response. They followed her voice to one of the offshoot rooms in the hallway.

Gwen was standing up from in front of an old corpse in the same kind of chamber the Oracle had been in. She slipped something into her pocket before coming out to Gerti and the councilman.

"So, are you a bear?" she asked.

"No. She's not." Emberlain replied. He turned to the guard and motioned for them to be escorted out.

Gerti and Gwen got a little ways from the science building before they talked freely.

"I didn't think I was gonna be able to work for them before but now I know. Their oracle is a mutated bear that's almost dead. It said its 'essence' wasn't alive or dead. That sounds pretty demonic to me." Gerti said.

"Essence? Like its spirit or something?"

"I guess." Gerti replied with a shrug. "All I need to know is that the Council basically worships it and it's not human. Did you feel anything weird in there?"

"No but I didn't try. I'm not used to thinking about it." Gwen said.

"That's fair. Maybe we can find someone to help you practice."

"I wouldn't even know where to start looking for that."

"Yeah. Well, I mean, that mayor."

"That's not funny." Gwen said through a laugh.

They passed out of the clean inner city to the dingy outer community buildings.

* * *

"Well," the girl began, "I did find something." She reached into her pocket and pulled out the black mirror. She had seen objects like this in the various ruins of her travels but she didn't know what they were. She handed it to Gerti and waited for any kind of response - waiting for Gerti to see the misty young man in the reflection but her expression never changed. She turned it over to look at the other side before giving it back.

"Looks cool. What is it?" Gerti asked.

"I don't know but did you not see him?"

"I'm sorry, what?" Gerti stopped walking and looked at the girl.

"When I first picked this up and looked at it. I saw a boy - I think it was the guy in the chair - asking me for help."

"That body you were next to?"

"Yeah."

"Uh, hey, Gwen. Just for future reference, when I asked if you felt anythin' weird, that definitely qualifies."

"I know, I just didn't want to say anything until we got out here." The girl looked at the smooth black surface and only saw herself. Where had he gone?

"Did he say what he needed help with?" Gerti asked, beginning to walk again.

"No. Are you not bothered by this?"

"I mean, of course I am but I don't know what all you can do. Maybe seein' ghosts is one of those things." Gerti paused, "I guess that would mean ghosts are real too? I might not've believed that before today."

"Either ghosts are real or I'm crazy," the girl said.

"Yeah, that's fair, I guess." Gerti said with a smile.

As they approached the clinic, a young man with a matured limp walked out of the doorway. He carried a small electric lantern that cast harsh blue light on his face.

"Hey Gerti! I heard you were back," the young man said.

"Hey Wendell. I got back this morning - I figured you'd be on the wall when I got here but I didn't see you. You visiting dad?"

"Uh, yeah. You know how it is," he replied, patting his damaged right leg. He kept his gaze on his leg for a few moments of silence before looking back up at them.

"Well hey, we're gonna go in and get dinner. Let's talk soon though." Gerti said.

Wendell nodded and passed them before turning off down an alleyway between mud and debris houses - his lantern illuminating an orb around him.

"That was awkward," the girl said quietly, after he had gotten out of earshot.

"Yeah. He had a crush on me when we were kids." Gerti replied.

"Ah. What happened to his leg?"

"He broke it when he was fourteen and it never set right. My dad still beats himself up over it."

They walked into the candle lit clinic. Gerti's dad was sitting at a desk in the living room looking over notes.

"I do," he said glumly.

"Sorry Dad. I didn't mean anything."

"Don't worry about it, Moonbeam. I know you didn't. Beating yourself up is part of the job. Y'all sit,

I'll get supper." He went into the old kitchen and started rummaging around.

"What do you mean - about your job?" the girl asked.

Luis Alvarez answered as he got their food together.

"I became the doctor because I wanted to help people. The only training I had was reading the books in the libraries here. We had a doctor before me but he was a drunk and got himself killed. So, I didn't have much in the way of a mentor. I lost a lot of people I should've been able to save. Wendell, the kid out there, his mother died when he was born." He came back in with two bowls of soup and sat down with them. He blinked hard a few times before continuing. "I was probably seventeen when Wendell was born. Elena was only a couple months from having Gerti. Anyway, I… she started hemorrhaging during the delivery and I wasn't able to do anything about it. So Wendell's dad ended up having to raise this kid on his own and that… didn't go well for either one of 'em. Dan didn't say two words to me through the day he died - and I really can't blame him." He wiped tears from his eyes.

"Dad, you've never told me that before."

"I've been thinking about it a lot lately," he said quietly. "I felt so powerless to save her. I can't even imagine how he must've felt just watching me. Whatever you do with the Council, please just be careful."

The girl didn't understand how the story connected back to the Council and the Oracle but she felt Mr. Alvarez did. Maybe he felt powerless to stop what was happening in front of him.

They ate dinner and called it a night.

Gerti's mom never joined them and her dad didn't know where she was. He had assured them that she does this sometimes and he was sure she was okay. The Alvarez's lived in the apartment above their clinic. It was the exact same layout as the unit below them except with the comforts of a home. They had old carpets hanging from the walls as insulation against the cold and dry Texas nights.

There was a small painted family portrait in a frame sitting on their kitchen counter. Gerti had been a tiny thing with a wide smile. Whoever painted it had done a good job - everyone was clearly identifiable. Gerti was a cute kid - it must have been before she got the scar on her face. Mr. Alvarez was clearly affable, and Mrs. Alvarez was as severe as she was in person. The girl was very impressed how their personalities could be so clearly captured by a handful of brush strokes.

Gerti's dad had set up a metal and nylon cot with thick blankets in their living room. She recognized it as being from the clinic's patient rooms. She smiled and laid down. After being on the road for so long, this was incredible. It wasn't as comfortable as Gloria's couch had been but it was a lot better than the plethora of abandoned houses she and Gerti had taken shelter in on their hike here. She laid in the dark apartment and let her mind wander.

She eventually landed back on the boy she had seen in the mirror earlier that day. The girl pulled it out of her pocket and stared at it. It was too dark to even see herself. She wondered if she even wanted to see him again. The girl felt like she should've been scared by him but she only felt curious. She finally gave up and put it back in her pocket before drifting off.

At some point in the night, she woke up, already sitting on the edge of her cot. She knew it was dark. Despite this, she was able to see in the room just fine. There were no shadows in the faint lambent flow of the room. She looked around. Partially peeled and cracked drywall, the bowls from dinner still on the table, her unconscious form lying on the cot, with the shallow breaths of sleep.

"Oh good," she said, quietly and somewhat bemused.

She looked around the room and saw a figure standing in the corner watching her.

The figure was silvery and moved like smoke caught in a dust devil - whipping back and forth. She looked closer - it was the boy. Boy probably wasn't the right term - he looked about her age.

"Hello?" she spoke quietly - not wanting to scare the ghostly mirage.

The figure didn't respond.

"You said you needed help. What do you need help with?" she asked.

"You can see me?" he asked, his voice was a faded whisper of his youth.

"Yeah," she hesitantly added, "Are you gonna hurt me?"

"No, of course not? I've been waiting for you - it's felt like forever."

"You've been waiting for me?" she asked, pointing at herself confused.

"I must've been. You're my angel of death, right?" he asked, taking a few steps towards her.

"I don't think I am. Are you a ghost?"

His face fell, and likewise, his frame collapsed onto the floor. He leaned against the wall behind him.

"But I've waited for so long. What year is it?" he asked.

"Twenty-one fourteen."

He looked shocked to hear this. Then his face screwed up and he started crying softly into hands. The girl got up from her cot and sat down beside the ephemeral figure.

"Hey, talk to me. Maybe me and my friend can help you." She placed a hand on his outstretched leg and was surprised she actually made contact with him. He stopped crying and looked at the place her hand rested. The ghost tilted his head in thought.

"It's been ninety years since I've felt someone touch me. I'd forgotten what it felt like." Tears began to well in his luminescent eyes again. "Everyone is gone," he said quietly between sobs.

"Hey, it's okay," she said, patting his leg, trying to reassure him. It was hard for the girl to know how long they sat like this. Time seemed to work differently here.

His tears eventually slowed.

"What's your name?" she asked, "Mine's… Gwen."

"Lance Conway." he muttered.

"Lance. It's nice to meet you Lance. You were alive before the fires? What's made you stick around?"

He nodded his head slowly and thought about how to answer the second question. The girl thought he looked like the working definition of forlorn.

"I was a student here before it all happened. I don't know for sure about the second thing. Well, I have a theory." The girl waited for him to continue. "I was working on a project that could move someone's mind into a machine. I was dying, so I uploaded my brain to keep going - God I wish I hadn't but I was so scared to die. I was alone for a couple months before I met any other people like me."

"Other people like you? I thought you were alone?"

"I had others for a few years before they kicked me out. It's okay, I didn't like them anyway. After they kicked me out, I wandered in the blackness until you picked up my phone and saw me."

She hadn't heard the term 'phone' before but she gathered that it was the black mirror.

"The blackness?"

"The area between life and death. It was terrible. Not because I was afraid or anything - I didn't feel like any of the things there could hurt me. It was terrible because I saw souls making their way to rest. I couldn't have that. I couldn't rest. I just want to close my eyes and sleep." He began to cry again.

They sat for another time, letting his tears dry while listening to the eerie silence of this odd ethereal version of the normal world they were sitting in.

"Who were the people you were with?" The girl asked.

"Some college admin who were able to hide deep enough before the fires swept through. God that was terrible too. You know, I actually died before the fires? Some asshole stabbed me and left me for dead. I was already gone when all those people burned. I saw all of them pass into the blackness."

"That sounds awful." The girl said.

"I was so scared - I didn't know what was happening. I wandered around campus for months before the people who survived came out. They were all starting to change into… monsters. I don't know how else to describe it. They thought they were dying and they all knew about my project. So they came to that building and uploaded their minds to the system. Every subject that did it, their body died twenty to thirty minutes afterwards. Even if the transfer was successful. They must not have read my reports thoroughly or else they would have known that. A lot of those people killed themselves before they realized what was happening to them. I tried to tell them about the angels but they didn't listen to me. All their souls moved on without them." He dropped his head into his hands before continuing.

"Because we were uploaded to the campus network, we had access to cameras and screens. I helped them explain to the other survivors that we were still alive, and how to use a live subject to bring us back into a living brain. I shouldn't have but I was afraid and just was trying to help them. The only one they could find was one of the old mascots for the school. I was horrified but at least they weren't using a person, I guess.

Anyway, those bears were so sweet, they would've gone anywhere their people took them. The president of the school was the first to try reuploading and Judge Rite was the first bear they used. That poor bear. It died as soon as they unplugged it from the frame - and so did the president. Judge Unum was the second. I suggested they leave it plugged in for longer to see how it affected the transfer. They never disconnected the second bear for fear it would kill us all. I don't know how but we had all seeped into the bear's head. For years we led a growing community from the bear's mouth. Eventually it took on a religious aura. I don't know why but I could still access the screens in the facility and talk to the people directly. They started calling me a prophet.

I thought it was kinda funny, because most of the people lost their faith in God entirely when they first caught a glimpse of the afterlife."

"What about you?"

"What do you mean?"

"You said they lost their faith - did you?"

"No, I actually felt better about it after I died. I had proof the afterlife existed at all. That's better than what I had before. And I saw angels coming to get the people who had died - angels just like in the paintings. Well, most of them were like the paintings."

The girl didn't know what paintings he was talking about but she kept listening. Lance's body had leaned over and his head rested on her shoulder as he talked.

"I've never seen the paintings you're talking about. What did they look like?"

"No? Well, they were tall - really tall - and they were wearing these long white robes that billowed when they flew to meet souls. I just wanted to go with them but they wouldn't take me. I tried asking them why but they wouldn't even speak to me. The other ones would - all they would say is that our time on Earth wasn't over yet. They said enough of me was still alive to keep me here."

"Who were the other ones - that talked to you?" the girl asked.

"I've never figured that out. They weren't around as much as the others."

"Why'd the others kick you out?"

"They, ugh, they started demanding the council bring people into the chambers to experiment with taking over their bodies. It got really dark. I told them I wouldn't help them - they were furious. They couldn't kill me, so they partitioned me to the room I was uploaded in. That's when I started to drift in the blackness."

"But you helped them with the bear. What was different about using a human?"

"I had some theories about a human's brain rejecting another mind being forced into it. That's not even mentioning the ethical and moral issues. I obviously never wanted to try - I don't know if they ever did though."

"So after all that, you just wanna give up and die?" the girl challenged.

"Whoa! Excuse me?" He leaned off her shoulder to look at her.

"They wanted to do horrible things and they wanted to make you help them. Then when you didn't, they put you in solitude for ninety-some-odd years - and you just want to let them win? From what my friend's told me, they still do horrible things to people here and are about to get a lot worse."

"I'm tired! I watched everyone I know die. I watched the world pass away while I was helpless and half dead. I just want to be done."

"There are people out here fighting them and they need help. Maybe you could help them and we could help you move on."

Lance sat up off the wall and appeared to be thinking it over.

"Okay fine. Deal - whatever. Whatever it takes to get me outta here. What do they need help with?"

"Well, could they transfer their minds to a robot instead of a living person?"

"Oh yeah, definitely - easy peasy. Digitizing a human's consciousness is easy - transferring it back to a living creature is more difficult for so many reasons. It's like trying to turn water into a computer program. Or reading aloud from a book and expecting the words to manifest. But, unless things have changed, it's a moot point. The only robots on campus were never activated."

"My friend and I brought back the program the robots needed to start."

"Oh, shit. Yeah, those will need to be destroyed before they figure out they can transfer to them."

"Gerti, my friend, said the Council was really excited about getting the program. So I think they already know, or maybe they're just planning on using them as soldiers."

"Either way, I think stopping them from controlling the robots is a good idea. Honestly, though, it might not be a problem. Do you know what version of the software y'all found?"

"I think it was two-eleven."

"Then we might not have to worry about them for long. The centaur bots can't handle that software for longer than about a month. They start losing their mind - I can't imagine that wouldn't affect a transferred conscience."

"How do you know so much about the robots?"

"I… I had a friend that worked on them before."

* * *

It was very early in the morning - still hours from sunrise.

Councilman Emberlain hadn't slept since Gertrude's meeting with the Oracle. Her irreverence had deeply troubled him. Emberlain was sitting alone at the Council table in the dark chamber. He mournfully looked at three of the empty seats. Darrowhill, Forestgate, and Alabatha had all been removed from their services as members of the Council. They had argued against the reviving of the Oracle for years but it had been academic before Gertrude retrieved the boot software. All three of them had been dear friends but the Oracle demanded their removal. He would miss them.

The Oracle was still apprehensive about transferring their minds to the robots after what happened with the bear all those years ago. Judge Rite - Emberlain corrected himself.

The doors to the chamber opened and Luis Alvarez was ushered in by two armor clad council-guards who were carrying advanced energy rifles.

"Luis, thank you for coming." Emberlain said.

Luis laughed genuinely amused but still ruefully. He took a seat in one of the empty chairs around the table. He smothered a smirk at the doctor brazenly taking a place at a table where he would never belong. He dismissed the guards. They were hesitant to leave the Councilman alone with the doctor - but they obeyed and left the room.

"I - The Council has an exciting proposition for you." Emberlain said.

Luis waited for him to continue.

"Do you feel as though you can perform at the level required by our community?" he asked.

"What do you mean?" Luis responded.

"I mean, do you feel adequate for the role you've found yourself in for the past twenty years?"

"If you have a complaint with my services -"

"No, not at all, Luis. I just worry that issues may arise that you won't be able to take care of in your current form. That you might need an edge to help the people of Waco."

"In my 'current form?' Councilman, what are you talking about?"

"The project your daughter was working on gave us access to robots from before the fires. The Oracle thinks they may have a way to give you control over the medical units - or at least one. They are capable of doing amazing things - miracles really."

"I know there's a catch."

"Not as much as you might think. You would be transferring your consciousness to a medical robot. Your body would die but your mind would live on forever in service of the Council and the Oracle. You would be able to use your skills to the absolute utmost to help our town. They can sew sutures in seconds, perform complicated brain surgeries, dispense medgel that can stop the most egregious wound from taking someone, and they are nearly indestructible - inexhaustible. I am truly jealous of this offer." Emberlain said, in total sincerity.

"Can't the robot do those things without me."

"It can perform basic tasks. Set a bone, plug a gunshot, things of that nature. The more complicated procedures require a human element."

"And I would die?"

"Your body would. Like I said, your mind would live on. You would become an immortal pillar of our community. An icon, dare I say, like the Oracle." Luis thought about it for a moment before standing up from the table.

"Immortal. huh?"

"Yes." Emberlain nodded. "And more powerful than you ever imagined. You would never fail another patient again."

Luis looked down at his hands. The same hands that had set bones, stitched wounds, and failed too many people. Too many children. He could save more. He could be better. Emberlain just needed him to see that too.

He took a breath and shook his head.

"No. No chance in hell. I'm not calling it quits until the good Lord calls me home. Is that all Emberlain?"

Emberlain controlled his temper as best as he could. Afterall, this man had saved the lives of most Council members at one point or another. Emberlain was no exception to that.

"You must be who your daughter gets her obstinance from."

Luis laughed heartily at this.

"That took teamwork from her mother and I," he said. "We are an unusually cantankerous family." Luis turned and exited the room without saying anything else to his superior.

The Councilman would not have described them that way. They were all mostly pleasant and friendly people - especially Luis.

However, he would concede they were a bunch of stubborn hairshirts. Emberlain felt pity for the man and his ignorant, antiquated beliefs. Sure, he knew the Oracle wasn't a god - but he also knew what the afterlife looked like and he knew it was nothing like what Luis believed. And to turn down an offer like this - the opportunity to serve the greater good…

Disappointed, he shook his head. The Council wouldn't have as much need for the outer community once the Oracle achieved machination. Everyone would eventually learn this.

Even still, in their infinite grace, the Oracle had extended invitations to some of the more desperate outer wall slummers. All they needed to do to receive their new vessels was to pledge earnest loyalty to the Council and to the god they served. Most turned their noses. Few of them were smart enough to agree.

Chapter Four
October 15th, 2114
Waco, Texas
Gertrude Alvarez

The following morning while scavenging in the heart of old Waco, Gwen told Gerti and Elena all the things Lance had said the night before. Gerti, somewhat embarrassed, realized she had forgotten to mention that part of her exchange with Emberlain and The Oracle. In haste, she recounted to Gwen and her mother about the Oracle planning on uploading themselves to the robots.

The three of them were moving slowly through an old shopping center in Waco. Burned out shells of old buildings lined the major highway intersection through the town.

"Lance said, the robots will go crazy after about a month if they run the software you brought back." Gwen said.

"Yeah, but then they'll just terrorize Waco the way they did in Bryan."

"Maybe we can sneak in and destroy the computers." Gwen said.

"The Council has that place completely locked up." Gerti's mom interjected. They had decided to take the day scavenging for the various items the Council paid good crystal to obtain.

"The Council guards have the Ferrell building locked down tight. I talked to some of the other fighters last night. They agree the robots need to be destroyed and have been working on a plan for us to get in there." Elena said.

"You're actually with the rebels now?" Gerti asked, digging through the trunk of an old car that looked like it had been passed over.

"Are you surprised?"

"No. I'm not surprised." Gerti took out a small broken tube of milky glass. She examined it closely before tilting the jagged edge into the palm of her hand. Three extremely small beads of shining silver rolled out into her palm. She smiled and put them in a plastic water bottle from her bag. Each bead of that size was worth a crystal on its own.

"I joined within hours of hearing they sent you away. I'm going to kill every single one of 'em for that. For what they did to my brother. For what they did to your grandparents."

"Well, I believe you about that." Gwen said.

"How many guards and bears do they have?" Gerti asked.

"Sixty-five Councilguard, and roughly eighty bears. We have sixty-two fighters."

"Are you going along with this?" Gwen turned and asked Gerti, jutting her thumb towards Gerti's mom.

She didn't feel like she had much of a choice - her mom was right in a lot of ways. The Council had done terrible things. Inhuman things. She looked Gwen in the eyes and nodded.

"You can count us in that number then." Gwen said to Elena.

"I already was," she responded while reaching down into the footwell of the car they were rummaging through.

She lifted out a human skull and jawbone. She examined the teeth closely - turning them around at every angle. She spotted what she wanted - dull metal embedded in the center of the teeth. She produced pliers from her pocket and pulled three teeth from the skull. Gerti held out the water bottle for her mom to store the teeth in.

"What exactly are we looking for?" Gwen asked, eyeing the procedure that just happened.

"I don't know what it's called. But the Council pays well for it." Gerti said.

They kept walking until they came to an odd shaped building - It was a massive black pyramid with a short facade on the front. It looked like a sideways rectangle with an odd bell shape in the middle of its flat facade. In the center of the building's facade, along the ground, there was a scorched concrete wall with a massive thick metal door sealing it shut. A hole had been cut through the door - large enough for a man to comfortably crawl through.

"I've seen this somewhere before." Gwen said, gesturing at the building's odd shape.

"It's a shelter." Elena explained. "People built them before the fires. This one got cut open."

"Have you been inside? I'm guessing it's been picked clean?" Gwen asked.

Elena and Gerti both nodded.

They moved on but Gerti noticed Gwen looking back occasionally at the opening until it was out of sight.

That afternoon, they exchanged what little they had found for crystals from the Council's buying agents. They managed to get nine from their light foray into old Waco.

Together, the three of them walked to Gropht's vegetable stand in the market. It was a short walk from the clinic, near the south wall out of Waco. He started packing up his stand's produce into a wheelbarrow when he saw the three women approaching him. He was done before they arrived - he motioned for them to follow. The wizened old man led them down several alleys to a nondescript earthen building tucked between two others just like it. Bricks and pieces of concrete were held together by hard packed clay from the river. There were three people inside the singular room, illuminated by the light that leaked through the holes in the sheet metal roof and the open door

Wendell Felder was sitting at a table fiddling with pieces of something metallic - Gerti couldn't tell what it was though. She wasn't surprised to see him here. He'd always had a rebellious streak.

His father was a drunk who beat him mercilessly for years - a behavior he corrected with a .38 when he was thirteen.

He nodded and smiled at Gerti when he saw her watching him. She recognized the other two but didn't know their names. A rough looking young man who's left arm was missing - burns twisted and distorted his flesh like melted wax. Scars like this weren't an uncommon sight.

The other was a woman who looked entirely ordinary. Gerti had only ever seen her at the market - usually at Gropht's trading homemade clothes for vegetables. The two were as unassuming as the building they were meeting in. Roughspun clothes repaired over the years with mismatched patches of fabric and different colored darning. They looked like everyone else in the outer wall community.

Wendell approached Gwen and Gerti carrying something. He held out Gerti's rifle to her and handed Gwen the rifle she had gotten from Jordan.

"I snuck them out of the armory. Y'all're gonna need 'em tonight."

"What are we doin' tonight?" Gerti asked.

"We're taking the Ferrell building," said the man who was missing his arm.

"What kind of resistance are y'all expecting?" Gerti asked.

"Hopefully very little." Elena answered. "They've increased security but we're planning on starting a dozen fires around town to draw their attention away. While we're doing that, you two will sneak in with Wendell and Clayton." Elena gestured at the burned man when she said Clayton.

"Clayton has electrical experience and has done work for the Council before. You have the most exposure to the robots and the most experience fighting them. I figured Gwen would want to go with you and Wendell insisted on going with you as well. I think between the four of you, y'all'll be able to either sneak in or talk your way past the guards. I'll leave that to your discretion." Elena said.

The four of them sat on a bench on the outskirts of the scrap-house neighborhood looking south to the gold domed building. Their weapons were stowed in the empty house at their backs. They were waiting for dusk and the distant pops of small arms fire to begin before moving.

There were patrols of silver clad council guards as well as green and gold adorned bears walking around the building. More than once a group stopped and asked what they were doing. They were able to wave off these questions fairly easily. Eventually, to avoid more suspicion, they went inside the empty house with their weapons. They didn't speak much while they were there.

Gwen was fidgeting, clearly wanting to talk but she kept quiet for a while until it eventually got to her.

"Read any good books lately?" she asked.

Gerti grinned. Had she forgotten about the laws against reading, or was she making a joke?

"No." Clayton said glumly. His left sleeve was pinned up over the stump of an arm. He looked preoccupied with his thoughts.

Gwen shuffled her feet on the blacktop flooring in the shack. Clayton leaned against the doorframe - positioned so he could keep an eye on the domed building. He tapped his hand rapidly on his leg.

"Wendell, Gerti told me you used to have a crush on her growing up - tell me about that." Gwen said.

"Whoa now." Gerti began "Wendell, you don't have to -"

"I don't mind talking about it," he said.

She shrugged and he continued.

"She was always calm and collected. And she always did what she thought was right even if it would've been easier not to. There was one time a girl, named Rose, came into town who had been injured. Her family had been killed and she managed to survive. I don't think she could've been much older than eight. Gertrude took off on her own to find the people who had attacked Rose's family. How old were you? Fourteen or fifteen?"

Gerti nodded. That had been a rough time - she tried not to think about it.

"She didn't know the girl - she didn't have to help. But she did. I admired her - I wanted to be more like her. I was inconsolable when she left - one, because I thought she was going to die, and two, because I was too scared to go after her."

"You had a lot going on at the time. And I didn't ask you to go with me." Gerti said. He had been dealing with his father. Neither job was fun or lighthearted.

"Yeah, but that's kinda my point. Nobody asked you to go out there either and you still did."

"What happened to Rose?" Gwen asked.

"She, and her adoptive family, left to settle a homestead somewhere north of here 'bout a year ago." Gerti answered.

"Will y'all be quiet?" Clayton asked.

"Why, you think you're gonna miss the gunshots just because we're talking?" Wendell asked.

"I just don't want to listen to you fawning over her anymore."

"Was I fawning? I didn't think I was fawning."

"I mean, you weren't professing your undying love or anything." Gerti said.

"I was interrupted," Wendell said with a laugh.

"Please stop." Clayton said with a scowl.

"Shall I also still my lips from likening your stony gaze to the summer storms that dominate the horizon? Dark, all-encompassing power that tears me down to my weakest, most raw being?" Wendell asked with a smirk towards Clayton.

"Dear God, Wendell. We're potentially moments away from dying. I need you - we need you to focus and stop being such a dumbass." Clayton said.

Gunshots began ringing off in the distance. Clayton pointed with his thumb towards the noise with a vindicated expression on his warped face. They all got up and checked their weapons over to make sure they were loaded. After a while the entire town sounded like a warzone. Energy weapons and deep large caliber reports were thundering at an almost constant rate. Once the patrols were away, the group moved - trying as best they could to press their weapons against their bodies to keep them obfuscated for as long as possible. The guards at the door raised their gleaming spears at the approaching group.

"Stop right there!" one yelled.

Everyone raised their rifles in response.

"Move aside. We're here for the robots, not you." Clayton said. His rifle was pinned between his right arm and torso, ready to fire.

"We'd rather die," one said.

"Those are your two options." Clayton said.

After a tense couple of seconds, the guards charged at the group.

Clayton squeezed off a few rounds from his single hand hipfire position, expecting the guards to go down. The bullets smacked the guards' antiquated plate armor.

They were unphased.

A spear lunged for Clayton but he twisted to the side - resulting in a glanced slice from the spear's blade. He let off a burst of rounds - one connected with the guard's exposed head and he went down with a charging force. The other took a long-armed swing at Gerti but Gwen put two bullets into his legs before he could follow through with the attack. He hit the ground with a groan - Clayton swiftly finished him off.

They moved through the front door into the outer ring of the old arena. It was cleaner than the last time Gerti had been in there but it was still as dark - they must've been saving power for the control station.

"Alright Alvarez, lead the way." Clayton said.

She led them to the control room. Nobody was manning the computers in the room - in fact nobody was in there at all.

"I'll keep watch, see what you can do." Clayton said to Gerti and Gwen. They set their rifles down and began looking through the computer. Wendell looked out in awe of the robots that were amassed in the massive arena. Gerti quickly realized she didn't know what she was looking for on the screen - Gwen stepped in to help.

"Ten pods of Trustee Bots, two medical units, and a Dullahan model." Gwen read aloud. Gerti assumed the Dullahan was the odd model out in the middle of the arena.

"Put your gun down, Wendell." Clayton said. Wendell turned around to see him pointing his rifle at him. He had already moved Gerti and Gwen's rifles away. Two council guards and four bears walked in and confiscated them. Gerti's heart sank.

Wendell white knuckled the trigger of his rifle and raked rounds across the whole lot of them. Some of them returned fire before falling. The deafening exchange ended in less than a second. The room filled with the smell of burnt gunpowder and blood. The report had deafened everyone.

Clayton and Wendell were unmoving on the ground. Three of the bears and one of the guards had fallen - the floor was quickly pooling with everyone's intermingling blood. Gerti lunged for a rifle on the ground but was struck by the boot of a council guard that was still upright. The impact sent her reeling into the control console.

She slipped in the bright red sanguineous drainage as she tried to right herself. Gwen moved to check on Wendell. She winced when the council guard yelled at her to stay where she was. Council Elder Emberlain walked in and waved away the gunsmoke in the air. He shook his head at all the bodies and looked upon the blood covered Gertrude with pity.

"I should have both of you killed right now. But you," He pointed to Gerti "I like your spirit. And you," He pointed to Gwen, "There's something about you the Oracle wants to utilize. Who am I to deny my master their desires? Get up so we can take you to them. Valens, check our man - we made a promise and we'll keep it if his state will permit it." He said the last to the council guard, who immediately moved to Clayton and began checking for signs of life.

A gunshot rang out that left the last bear's gray matter sprayed against the wall of the control center. Two more gunshots leveled the startled Emberlain.

Wendell had drawn his .38 revolver and with every ounce of his strength, used it to give them another chance. The council guard stood to finish Wendell off but was interrupted violently by Gwen. She had grabbed the object nearest her, a faded gold and green ceramic mug, and began reducing it to jagged and shattered pieces against the council guard's exposed face. She screamed like a feral banshee as he went down - three quarters of her now covered in his blood. She didn't stop until the only survivors of the immediate conflict were herself and the mug's crescent handle in her hand.

Gerti scrambled to her feet and went to Wendell. Bright red blood soaked the fabric of his pants high on his right thigh where a bullet had torn. Another round had pierced his right cheek - leaving it a fleshy flap. It had narrowly missed so many things that would have resulted in his immediate death. Any garnered luck denoted by that fact was negated by the gushing arterial blood from his thigh. She pressed into the wound on his thigh with all her might, trying to stop the bleeding.

"Gwen! I need help! I need a tourniquet!" she cried. There wasn't an answer. "Gwen!" she cried again.

She turned to see Gwen holding the guard's glistening spear - its bladed tip lifting Emberlain's chin up. He was laid prone, whimpering as he looked into Gwen's eyes.

"Gwen!" She looked back at Gerti, her eyes were a lifeless, unfocused gray.

With one quick motion she drove the spear out through the back of Emberlain's skull. She released the shaft and it wobbled down a little before sticking, lodged in the spine of the dead council member. His head lolled to the side causing the spear to bounce off the concrete floor.

She removed the leather belt she was wearing and bent down to place it around Wendell's thigh above the wound. She cinched it as tight as she could and marked a line in the leather. She pulled it loose and punctured a hole with a small knife from her pocket. She put her body weight into cinching it down again and securing it. She did this deftly and with a cool, expressionless look on her face. It chilled Gerti to her core. She had only seen such animalistic violence one other time in her life and it was not a time she tried to revisit. She shook these thoughts from her head and tried to triage the situation.

Wendell's bleeding was staunched so she retrieved her rifle and drove the butt of it into the computer towers attached to the control console. The screens blinked out to signal loss - she hoped that was enough. She and Gwen helped Wendell to his feet and the three of them made their way to the Alvarez' clinic. The twilight air was already beginning to cool from the heat of the day. Gunfights could still be heard all around them - mostly from the council's inner wall district.

* * *

Elena rocked a magazine into the receiver of her rifle and racked the bolt handle on the right side. A satisfying thunk told her a round was in the chamber. She popped out the side of the concrete cover she was behind and settled her sights on a council guard who had paused to slot a new power cell into his energy rifle. Three .30 caliber rounds from her rifle hit his chest plate like rapid fire hammer strikes. He hit the ground - his rifle landed away from him. A chunk of her cover turned to a puff of dust and rocky debris. She slid back behind the stone embankment. Whoever the architect was that designed this campus probably never expected their decorative spaces to be used as a trench wall by her and a handful of her comrades.

A Council guard holding a large square shield and a spear came around the corner of the divider furthest from her. One of the fighters close by lost his footing and fell. Bullets impacted the shield to no effect. The guard yelled a battle cry as he stabbed down at the fighter. His gunfire was cut off and replaced with a scream of pain. The guard quickly killed the other fighter that was next to the first - she hardly saw it coming. Then he turned his attention to Elena.

She put a few rounds into the shield. The guard continued his advance. She tried to place rounds somewhere more effective but everything was covered by the glimmering silver armor. She looked around for other fighters but she was alone.

The guard feigned several attacks before finally committing to a full lunge. Elena twisted to dodge and grabbed the spear's shaft. She pulled it as hard as she could to throw the guard's balance off. He over-extended and exposed his unarmored head. She would take every opportunity she could. It was sloppy, one-handed work, but she let off a burst of full auto and at least one round made its mark.

The guard slumped back, lifeless. Seeing another opportunity, she unlimbered the shield from the guard's wrist and attached it to her own. She quickly took stock of her surroundings just in time to see two-armed council guards come around the embankment where she had been a few moments earlier. Their weapon's energy bolts lit the ground in a sinister red as they scorched their path.

She instinctively lifted the shield to meet the bolts. It absorbed the blasts with almost no reverberation. She hefted her rifle around the side of the shield and laid into the two guards. As they went down, she felt a deep burning pain in her side. A spear tip was sticking out of her abdomen from the back.

Elena pulled away and turned to her new attacker - the pain was excruciating. She leveled her rifle and pulled the trigger. The firing pin struck an empty chamber. The guard rammed her with his shield and she hit the ground hard - cracking her skull on the pavement.

* * *

Luis Alvarez had set up a temporary medical suite, if you were loose with the application of the term, in a house a little ways away from his main clinic. Everyone knew there would be an influx of wounded fighters and he didn't want them all getting dragged back to his home. Even still, fighters were bringing their wounded in like ants. If the Council wanted to find them, it wouldn't be difficult. He was thankful most of the wounded had received preliminary first aid, tourniquets, bandages, etc. It made his job of triage a little easier.

Right now, he was diligently suturing the femoral artery in Wendell's leg. He was proud of everyone's handling of the wounds they were presented with -

bandages were clean, tourniquets were tight. Even while they waited for his care, some had taken to cleaning and dressing the less severe wounds. The last of the gunshots outside had stopped several minutes ago.

He wondered how many people had died and if it was worth it. Gerti said they were successful in destroying the computers but she wasn't sure that would be enough.

* * *

Gerti nestled her rifle on the handrail and braced it against the corner support pipe on the second story balcony of their apartment building. Metal plates and tin cans full of sand had been piled up to make cover between the open metal railing. She and Gwen had a good vantage point of her dad's field clinic.

It was in an earthen hut built on the remnants of the double street running north-south. The Ferrell building in the distance. The entrance was facing her and was, at most, forty yards from her muzzle - close enough she was confident she could hit anyone the Council sent.

They had dropped Wendell off and were now acting as a rearguard for the retreating fighters. She strained her eyes to watch for signs of attackers in the darkness. Glimpses of motion, flickering running lights on their energy weapons, anything.

To Gerti's surprise, it didn't seem like the Council guards, or the bears, were interested in following the fighters. They watched from their perch for several hours. The trickle of people eventually faded to nothing.

Something started to pester Gerti's mind - where was her mother? She reminded herself that her mother could've slipped in and she would never have known. The thought that she could be dead or incapacitated didn't enter Gerti's mind for a moment.

Gwen was sitting on the floor of the concrete balcony with her back to the apartment's wall. Her rifle was laying next to her right side and she was staring off into the middle distance. The blood that covered her had dried brown and had begun flaking off her skin.

"You okay?" Gerti asked quietly. It had been hours since she had spoken and her voice caught in her dry throat.

Gwen slowly nodded her head - barely paying attention.

"It's gonna be a long night if you want to go inside and get some rest." Gerti offered.

"You sure?"

Gerti nodded and motioned for Gwen to go inside.

"If I need you out here, I'll shoot to wake you up." Gerti said with a grin.

* * *

The girl laid down on the cot Mr. Alvarez had made up for her. The entire trip up to Waco, she had spent every night trying to focus on her abilities - they came easier right before sleep. There were some nights she felt like she had forgotten how to fall asleep normally because she would get too excited about trying to broaden her abilities.

She closed her eyes and listened to the ocean waves that coursed in her mind as her brain tried to interpret the ringing in her ears. She felt her mind wander to what she could remember of her home back east and the people that had surrounded her there. The blood she had seen and the things she had learned to do. Like the things she had done to that council guard and Emberlain.

She envisioned the powerful waves she had seen crash into the shore of the gulf beaches. Her waking mind didn't have the key to these memories - she never knew why or how she was capable of such violence. She deeply wanted to remember, to make sense of the blank spots in her mind.

She felt herself moving with the shifting tide of her mind. There was an untraversable chasm between her conscious and unconscious and she deeply yearned to bridge it. She had always held the idea that a person was a culmination of their choices and actions. Could she be whole if she wasn't able to remember?

She shifted under her blanket and felt dried blood flake off her arm. Her last conscious thought was that she'd have to clean the blankets when she woke up to avoid being a bad guest. She felt a warm comforting hand settle on hers. She sat up to see who had come in so silently. Lance was sitting on the edge of her cot - a worried expression on his face.

"You okay, Gwen?" he asked.

She smiled, liking the sound of that name for the first time.

Chapter Five
October 16th, 2114
Bryan, Texas
Joseph Marion

Joe had worked late into the night again. The Bryan motor pool had basically become his new home. Purcevale, Joe's two-tailed cat, had even picked up on this change and had begun hanging around there instead of his apartment.

The motor pool was an old brick fire station they had cleared out to store their handful of vehicles, along with the Trustee Bots from the campus. The vehicles had been moved to the parking garage to make room for the expanding mess of robot parts that now covered every section of the floor.

A damaged Trustee Bot was splayed out on the bare concrete floor. The bot sat on its plastic case belly - torso upright holding a wooden 2x4 instead of its energy rifle. Someone, (Gloria) had used a pencil to colorfully denote which end of the warped 2x4 was the business end. The bot's trunks of multicolored wiring pulled out and split. They dangled freely like the branches of the willow trees that still grew around the old lake. Only a handful of those wires were still attached to a Treighl Industries circuit board.

Joe was carefully soldering wires onto the maze of golden circuit traces. A small screen laid on the floor with a rainbow of wires connecting it to the bot. An array of switches laid beside him - some were already connected to the board. He finished soldering the lead he had made to the spade terminal on a switch and pressed it down. The bot's torso twitched left twenty degrees and stopped abruptly when he released pressure. He picked up another switch and repeated the process in reverse. He repeated the process, this time watching the screen next to him to make sure the feed from the bot's cameras kept pace.

It did.

Joe could've sworn he felt a tear start to well. He had done something similar with a piece of construction equipment last year for Danny but he wasn't sure he'd be able with a machine this advanced. Something must've been in the air, because he got more emotional wishing his brother could be there to see how far he had come. He chalked it up to lack of sleep - or stress. Little column A, little column B. He stood up and stretched. He had been sitting on the floor for hours by then. There was a boot-shuffle of grit on concrete behind him. Joe started and spun around.

"Yeah!" Allen yelled in an almost yee-hawing cadence and energy that made Joe jump.

"You're gonna get shot if you keep doing that." Joe said.

Allen laughed.

"I've been standing here for a while. You should lock the door. What are you doing up this late?" he asked.

Joe motioned vaguely towards the Trustee Bot.

"I got the controls and camera working - just need to figure out how to make it shoot."

"How's your dog doing?" Allen asked.

Joe sighed forlornly and looked over at the trooper bot curled up on one of the workbenches. Her shell was stripped, exposing the complicated compact inner workings of the canine robot. Purcevale sniffed around the dead metal.

"No progress."

"Well, keep workin' at it." He checked his wrist watch. "But you should get some sleep. You won't be any good tomorrow."

"What's tomorrow?"

"Work." Allen said, laughing. "Get some sleep. This'll be here tomorrow." Allen walked towards the exit but turned around again. "We're having a meeting tomorrow, me, Jacob, Willow, an' Pastor. Same spot and time as usual. I want you to be there too. We're talkin' about where to take the leadership from here."

"You tired of being in charge already?" Joe asked.

"Yes." Allen said without hesitation. "Goodnight Joe."

"G'night Allen."

Allen had always been a live and let live kind of guy and that fit well with Joe. The thought of someone else being in complete charge was worrisome. He knew if it came to a public vote, Allen would most likely be the one selected. He figured Jacob would run - but too many people had gotten crossways with him over the years. Willow was still trying to regain people's trust from having worked with Frank for so many years and he doubted the pastor would want the job.

Joe walked into a little office space on the outer wall of the fire station that he had set up as his sleeping area. A spare sheet over a dilapidated couch that survived the fires. He laid there thinking about the crazy stuff he had lived through in the last month. He wondered how Gerti and Gwen were doing. These thoughts carried him off to sleep.

The next morning, Joe met Gloria at the cafe for breakfast before heading off to find Allen. They eventually found him in the park across from the old theater - next to Harold's old barbershop. Allen and Pastor Gene were already there talking at a stone table.

The pastor had been mentoring Allen every Tuesday morning for several years now. Other people had come and gone from these weekly meetings, even Joe on occasion, but Allen and Pastor Gene were the constants. An old leather Bible sat on the table between them.

Joe sat down - there were enough seats for everyone else that was supposed to be there that morning. They said good morning and continued to the end of their conversation. Speaking of a section in Proverbs that talked about the inclinations of a wise man versus those of a fool. Willow and Jacob joined them while they were wrapping up.

“I’d like to say a prayer before we begin.” Pastor offered.

At their approval he bowed his head and continued. Joe had never been comfortable with public prayers like this - it always seemed performative at best. But he bowed his head and listened to the pastor’s words.

“Dear heavenly Father, thank you for allowing us another warm sunrise in this harsh world. The book of Lucas says anyone seeking wisdom should come to you and that you would give it generously.”

Joe opened his eyes to peek at the people at the table. Willow was staring down at the table.

“We’re coming before you today asking for this generous wisdom. We’re asking for guidance on how to lead this community with strength, integrity, and righteousness. For your glory, we want to be your shining city on the hill of this dark, dark world so all may see the light of your love and grace. It's in your name we pray, amen." Pastor Gene finished and lifted his head.

"So, where do we begin?" he asked.

"Succession. We've all been holding down the fort. We either need to find a leader to oversee everything going on in the community or we need to figure something else out." Allen began, "In the past, Frank was solely in charge and that led to a lot of awful things. Willow, do you have any suggestions how we could avoid that moving forward?"

"Well, I say we keep operatin' the same way we did when Frank was in charge - just without Frank," she said.

"What do you mean?" Jacob asked.

"You stay in charge of security, Allen stays in charge of maintenance, maybe we bring in Mrs. Laredo, or an elected position, as a community rep." Willow said.

"That'll keep the bad ideas scattered… compartmentalized. Less chance for one bad apple running the show." Joe said, nodding.

"Like a council." Pastor said, "I could see that working. Would we elect each position or continue with what we have?"

"Let's cross those bridges when we need to." Jacob said.

"Well okay, should we vote on this or something?" Allen asked.

"I don't hear any dissenting opinions." Pastor said, looking around at everyone.

They all nodded.

"Okay, then it sounds like we have a plan. We stay business as usual with the exception of a town representative instead of a mayor." Pastor said.

* * *

It was early morning when Marcus hauled the rebel woman onto a metal pull cart. The hair on her head was matted with blood from a nasty head wound. That must've been what did her in. He removed the silversteel shield from her arm - It probably came off of Carnegie, who had laid dead mere feet from her before someone carried his corpse off. He pulled her body to the gate in the wall that separated the outer slums from the Council sector. Marcus lifted her up and placed her in rank with the other dead rebels he and the other guards had rounded up.

Every Council guard his order had to spare was present. Some were transporting the dead but most were standing alert with their energy rifles ready to bear. The day was already heating up and sweat was beginning to bead under his armor.

He shook his head as he looked at the dead rebels. What had they died for? There wasn't a need for them to attack the Council like this. He wiped the sweat from his forehead and began walking back to look for more dead or injured. An older, gray haired, bear by the name of Chris Riggans climbed the rampart of the dividing wall. He held a conical device in his hand that he held up to his mouth.

"The Council and the Oracle wish to end our hostilities. Your dead, from last night's attack, have been laid by the main gate. We would like to retrieve our injured. We kindly request a cease fire," he said, his voice magnified. "We're sending unarmed bears out for this purpose." He finished and climbed down again.

Marcus had mustered into the ranks of Council Guard nearly three months prior. His mother had cried because it meant he would have to patrol the outer slums. His father welled with pride. He had been issued a light set of silversteel armor and silversteel spear - known to be the strongest metal they had. Even the light armor was capable of stopping small arms fire. Its creation was a blessing from the Oracle themself.

He said a quick prayer of thanks to the Oracle and asked for their protection as he executed their will.

A group of bears gathered by the main gate and were sent out. He felt his face twist with disgust for a moment before he consciously cleared it. Bears were slummers but they had been cleared by the Council and by the Oracle. He said a prayer of forgiveness for his moment of weakness and judgment.

His captain, Bartholomew, approached him with two other guards from his cohort. Bartholomew had been in the guard for a long time. Marcus counted himself lucky to be under the charge of such an experienced man. He had an energy rifle slung over his shoulder and was carrying a second cradled in his arms. He held it, and a small musette bag of energy cells, out to Marcus. Guards were issued spears at the start of their assignment and were normally required to prove themselves before they earned these rare and powerful weapons. He hesitantly took both and slung them over his shoulder.

"Councilwoman Stribley has assigned us to secure the Ferrell building. We're to shoot any resistance on sight. Clear?" Bartholomew asked.

The honorable Councilwoman Stribley was standing on an elevated concrete walkway overseeing the work. Her green robes, and gray hair, swaying elegantly in the morning breeze. The very picture of regality.

"Yessir." Marcus wasn't sure he was ready for that kind of task. But if the Council thought he was ready then he must be. They waited for the slummers to come get their dead before heading out. More than generous, he thought. They were disgusting - threadbare clothes and dirty skin. Ratty hair, scars. Marcus said no prayer of forgiveness for these thoughts.

One of the young women, wearing bear colors no less, let out a gut-wrenching cry when she saw the woman Marcus had hauled into the lineup. He had a moment of remorse but he reminded himself they started this fight and they should've been ready for the consequences.

* * *

Gerti fell down beside her mother's body. Gwen bent down beside her and checked her mother's pulse. Luis had worked on people in the jaws of death - but it had never been his wife.

"She's still alive." Gwen whispered. She looked around and called for Mr. Alvarez, who was already hurrying over to them. Gwen patted Gerti on the shoulder.

"Hey, focus up," Gwen said firmly. They carefully hauled Elena up onto a cart.

"Beth," Luis said to his assistant, "stay here, find any survivors and organize retrieving the dead. I have to -"

"Go, go. I'll take care of this." Beth motioned for him to leave and do what he needed to do.

"Careful to keep her head straight," Mr. Alvarez instructed, as they rushed Elena to the clinic.

They lifted her onto a bed and immediately, he felt for a pulse to confirm what Gwen had said. He grabbed a bottle of liquor and carefully rinsed the blood out from around her wound. He felt around for a fracture. His stomach fell out when he felt loose fragments of her skull moving under her scalp. He took a deep breath and prayed silently.

"Hold her head," he told Gerti. She took his place as he began looking for scissors and his shaving kit. He carefully and quickly trimmed and shaved her head around the wound. The scalp around the wound was swollen and distended.

He needed copious amounts of disinfectants and a way to relieve the pressure in her skull. He didn't have the equipment or experience to deal with this. His heart sank when he realized what he needed to do.

"Gwen, take over for Gerti." His voice caught as he spoke. "I need to speak with her." They stepped away and he embraced her in a tight hug.

"I love you, Moonbeam," he said quietly.

"I know Dad, I love you too. Is Mom not going to make it?" she asked.

"I think she can but I'll need to take some drastic measures. Emberlain offered me a chance to upload my brain to one of those robots - the medical unit. He said it can perform complicated surgeries. My body will die but I'll live on and your mother will live too."

"Dad, you'll lose your mind after a month. The programming is messed up. And Emberlain is dead."

"The Council would've known about his offer. And you'll have time to figure that last bit out. Your mom's not going to make it much longer - it's a miracle she's still alive as it is."

Gerti wanted to ask her dad to not go but she bit it back and nodded.

"Okay then. Do you want us to come with you?"

"I think it's better if you stay here with your mother." Luis didn't want to make his daughter watch him die. She nodded, wiped tears from her eyes, and hugged him tight again before he left.

* * *

Bartholomew led his cohort through the dirty streets of the outer slums towards the Ferrell building. Their rifles scanned every window and doorway as they moved. Every guard walked while constantly being aware of any piece of hard cover they might have to use in case of an ambush.

The Ferrell building was only a thousand feet from the Bagby gate. Marcus felt like every inch of this horrible place was going to try to kill him. Every door hid a rebel - every window was a gunport. A door burst open from one of the southern apartment buildings and a portly man came running at them. He was unarmed. It took a moment but Marcus recognized him as Dr. Alvarez - possibly the only slummer that held almost universal respect on both sides of the dividing wall. The cohort all held their fire as the doctor approached them. He wasn't the type to fight.

"I need to speak to a council member," he said out of breath. Bartholomew owed a great deal to the doctor - they all did. He nodded in agreement.

"Marcus. Take Doctor Alvarez to Councilwoman Stribley. Radio into Justin if there's trouble." Bartholomew gestured to their radioman.

Marcus nodded acknowledgment and began leading the doctor back to the gate. They weren't far. People on the other side of the wall gave them quizzical looks until they recognized the doctor. Stribley looked down from her overwatch - her expression softening as Dr. Alvarez approached.

"I'm here to accept the Council's offer. My - I have a patient with severe head trauma that I can't help without the robot. I'm sure you have injuries that need extreme medical aid as well." He was still out of breath.

"We have a cohort going to secure the Ferrell building. We will radio them to bring the medical unit back to the Oracle so we can begin transfer. In fact," she began to call out to the guards gathered around the yard, "Ferinal, Terris, take your cohorts to the Ferrell center to reinforce Bartholomew's. Relay that they are ordered to bring a medical unit, and standard unit, back to the Oracle immediately." She stepped down and took the doctor's hands into her own. "I'm glad you've decided to join us," she said softly. Marcus was thankful the Councilmembers were such affable and upright people. Mr. Alvarez was a good man and the Council was good for helping him.

"Marcus, take Luis to the Oracle and have the priests prepare him for the ceremony. You know where the Oracle is, yes?" she asked.

"Yes Ma'am," he said dumbly. He had never been inside there and he had certainly never seen the Oracle. His head swirled with the rapid changes going on in his career. He led the doctor to the Marrs Science Building though he didn't know where to go once inside.

Thankfully there was a priest there he could ask. It was a former guard who had ascended in honor to the rank of priest - an honor guard of the Oracle. He led them through the halls towards the Oracle's chamber. He was almost giddy with each set of doors they passed through - each set of green and gold banners they passed beneath.

* * *

Luis' heart was racing. Every fiber told him this was a bad idea but he knew it was what he needed to do to save Elena. He wasn't going to let her die.

The guard escorting him was smiling from ear to ear like a dumb kid - looking all around him. Luis felt bad for what he was about to find out of his godly Oracle. The scent of rot was already filling Luis' nostrils - the kid didn't seem to notice. Marcus, Luis thought. That was his name. His mom had brought him into the clinic for a fever of a hundred and five when he was eight or nine. How long ago that felt.

The metal double doors at the end of the old hallway creaked open to reveal the candlelit room where the Oracle resided. He had heard descriptions of the beast from Gerti but it didn't stack up to the horrors his own eyes saw now. The smile on Marcus' face was gone - wiped off by the rotting smell that washed out into the hallway like a gust of poison. Luis and Marcus stepped into the chamber. The doors were closed behind him by two of the Oracle's priests.

"Please take a seat so I can prepare you for the ritual." The priest gestured to an office chair that had been adorned with ornate ribbons. Luis did so. The priests stood behind the chair and began trimming the hair from his head. There was another outer wall citizen sitting next to him. He was already seated in a chair - shaved and read for transfer. He was covered in blood, was missing an arm, and was barely hanging onto life. It was Clayton. Mr. Alvarez recognized him from when he had to cauterize the stump of his arm.

"The spirit of the Prophet left clear instructions on the steps to take before ascension." The priest spoke in a deep, low voice. "Your head must be unencumbered and clean shaven so as to connect to the spirit world more easily. A faulty connection could lose your soul in between our world and the Oracle's. An unimaginable loss that would be." Electric trimmers ran over Luis' head, followed by lathered soap and a single blade. Tears in Luis' eyes caught the soft glow of the candlelight.

"Now that you are ready, please take a seat at the right hand of the Oracle. So you may serve them until the second fires come and wipe the world clean again," the priest said.

Luis knew a religion had formed around this abomination but he had no idea what the priest was talking about. He had one thing on his mind. He moved to the pod seat next to the puss filled bear corpse. Marcus looked on, horrified.

"I must anoint your head for the transfer," the priest said, holding a glass jar of some viscous fluid.

Luis nodded.

The priest began lathering a thin layer of the jelly onto his bare scalp. He looked Luis in the eyes as he lowered a cabled crown onto his head. He pressed down on the crown's pads.

"How lucky you are," he said.

Luis could hear the genuine jealousy in the priest's voice. The double doors opened again and two Trustee Bots walked in. The medical unit had a white plastic outer casing with a red cross across its chest. Its white case absorbed the warm light from the flickering candles. It was walked up to the station by two guards and a priest. They connected it to one of the machines in the computer bank with a thick trunk of cables. The priest tending to the robot gave a thumbs up to the priest helping Luis. He nodded.

Luis said a prayer he knew would be his last. He poured out as much of his soul as he could in the little time he had left - bittersweet tears streamed down from his closed eyes.

The only image in his mind's eye was his wife and little girl. It was a warm winter day. They had taken the day to celebrate something, he couldn't remember what, but he remembered the day had been perfect.

The priest at the computer pressed a series of buttons and the lights went out for Luis. He was standing in an endless void of nothingness. He looked around for a sign of anything. He could only sense the faint outline of the room he had been in though it was already fading into non-existence.

"Luis Alvarez," a commanding voice made Luis jump at first. He wasn't scared though - just surprised. A warm and loving hand reached out to guide him.

"You've done enough. It's time to come home, Luis."

Chapter Six
October 16th, 2114
US Highway 249, Southbound
Brandon Clements

In theory, it should've only been a fourteen hour walk from the Fairegrounds to the village of Jersey in the kingdom of Houston. In reality, their troop was moving slowly and full of caution. The black dragon still roamed the skies and the land was still fraught with countless dangers. They had been on the road for several days at this point.

The group of adventurers crawled out from under a broken piece of highway overpass. They had been on the road for three days now - often having to stop to avoid the dragon. There were other smaller robots that patrolled this area as well. Smaller was a relative term, in relation to the dragon.

They were a little larger than a full-grown man. Angular heads that were narrower than a man's. They had metal shells that had been painted green before the fires. Brandon Clements figured they must have been military issued - it looked like it had been that olive drab green he saw in old recruiting pamphlets at the university. Swane and the other warriors from the Fairegrounds referred to them as orc droids. Whatever kept their fantastical view of the world going.

He climbed out of the rubble that had covered the entrance to their overpass camping spot the night before. He turned around to help his new friend, Francis, out of the same hole. They were both wearing the brown robes, tied together with electrical wires, that denoted their position in the technomancy order. Francis and Brandon were still acolytes who were required to bring a new piece of technology in for study. Francis had been on the cusp of achieving this when his group met Brandon - but it slipped from his fingers. They both figured whatever lair this dragon called home would have plenty of advanced tech for retrieval.

Swane's band of warriors were in it for the toil of the hunt and the glory of the kill.

Swane 'The Pain Train' led a group of eccentric warriors who all carried antiquated medieval weaponry. To be fair, Brandon had seen these fighters use their odd weapons with extreme proficiency.

Swane carried a massive two-handed claymore that he kept racked on his back. He was the most fearsome - a mass of muscle who, unarmed, would still be formidable against most threats in the wasteland. He wore a red hoodie and a kilt with red high top converse shoes that were frayed at the top. His blonde hair was in a mullet and he sported a thick handlebar mustache. Brandon thought he looked ridiculous but he wasn't going to say that to Swane's face any time soon. Besides, it was among the least ridiculous things about him.

Galahad carried a glimmering shield he said was made of mithril, and a steel longsword. Morgana, was a thin woman who wore a hiked up purple and black dress and carried a bow. He had never seen her draw it the whole time they had been out here. Swane said she was a skilled sorceress and that was her main weapon.

Had someone said that to Brandon three weeks ago, he would've called them crazy. But the people of the Fairegrounds did seem to have some measure of magic - if you could believe that. The two scouts guiding them to the village of Jersey were named Godfried and Halifax. They seemed the most normal to Brandon. Even still though, they carried compound bows and wore leather armor that had been dyed in mottled patterns with dark paints for camouflage.

As for Brandon and Francis, they stuck to tried and true twentieth century revolvers. Brandon thumbed the cylinder of his old mentor's gun and wondered how he and his family were doing back at the university. The last member of their party was a man named Talon. Brandon had to assume that was a self-assigned moniker because who would name their sweet little baby something so edgy? Though to be fair, Talon looked rough enough one might assume he never had been a sweet little baby. He was a young man with thick black hair. His limbs had been replaced with mechanical appendages. They were gunmetal gray metal and black carbon fiber panels where there should have been skin. His right forearm was simply a cannon whose maw glowed a faint red whenever it was spinning up to fire. Talon had insisted on joining them on their journey but hadn't said why. Brandon was thankful to have a walking cannon on his side.

Brandon chuckled to himself thinking of how he had come to be part of such an unlikely group. He suddenly stopped smiling- growing somber when he remembered their quest was to slay a pre-fire military grade killing machine.

He hiked up his backpack and kept trudging down the highway. Halifax held up a hand for them to stop and listen. There was a droning buzz of insects. Embedded therein was a deeper throbbing of heavier wingbeats.

"Weapons out." Godfried said calmly. They all unlimbered their weapons and prepared for what they hadn't yet seen.

"What is it, Brother?" Swane asked.

"Bloodwraiths. I don't know how many," he replied.

As he finished speaking, five fuzzy black insects the size of large dogs hovered up from behind the other side of the overpass they were on. Six dangly legs hung underneath fat abdomens. Each had a long snout the size, length, and thickness of a broom handle sticking out of their ugly faces.

Brandon aimed his revolver but the creatures darted back and forth as they closed the distance - it was hard to draw a good bead on them. Swane and Galahad met them halfway, cleaving two into pieces. Blood splashed out of them and fell to the ground with wet splats. Morgana said something in a language Brandon wasn't equipped to understand. Two more of the creatures exploded in a bloody mess. The last one was evaporated by a thumping energy bolt from Talon's arm cannon. The deep throbbing was thankfully absent from the cacophony of insects.

"Stay vigilant, Brothers." Swane advised as he racked his massive sword.

They continued down the old highway. Bare trunks of long dead trees filled either side of the roadway. The rest of the day consisted of them avoiding a patrol of ork droids and taking cover from the dragon for probably thirty minutes. They were reassured that the dragon headed South-East once its patrol was up. They came across a highway intersection with plenty of buildings to camp in for the night. A large metal building with a caved in roof was what they landed on. They found offices in the back that would act as enough concealment for them. Their scouts estimated they'd arrive the next day - if everything stayed this level of smooth.

* * *

The whole town of Bryan had been called to assemble at the old brick church. Pastor Gene stood at the pulpit and waited for everyone to settle into their seats before he began. He opened with another reverent prayer before explaining the contents of the meeting that morning. Everyone seemed to think this would be a reasonable course of actions after what happened with the mayor. Of course nobody voiced that - the late mayor's wife and kids were in attendance and to do so would be unbecoming of polite society.

"In regards to the community representative; the name that popped out to us was Mrs. Laredo. But obviously her involvement is entirely up to her and we wanted to encourage a vote."

"I think I could do that." Mrs. Laredo said from the crowd.

"Okay, does anyone else want the position?" Nobody spoke up. "Ayes have it then?" he asked. Everyone nodded their head or otherwise made congenial motions. The pastor laughed. "Hallelujah. Here I was, thinkin' government would be a difficult affair."

The congregation laughed politely.

* * *

The door to the Alvarez' clinic slowly swung open. Gerti and Gwen turned to look. The white bodied medical Trustee Bot strolled into the room - its head almost touched the ceiling of the apartment. It walked up to Elena, one hand held her head rock steady. The other hand produced a drill from its index finger. It started spinning with a high pitch whine. The robot drilled into the wound in her head and used a vacuum to extract any bone dust and debris. It then dropped its hand at the wrist and loaded a canister of medgel. It secreted a thin layer of the medgel around the wound then wrapped her head in gauze, making sure to leave holes for her eyes, and nostrils. Afterwards, it laid her head down gently on a pillow.

"Two weeks recovery time. Patient should regain consciousness in a matter of hours. She is to be kept off her feet for the full two weeks," the robot said this in the same kind female voice used by the one on the campus that had tried to heal Gwen. The robot turned its attention to Wendell. It removed the bandages, applied medgel and applied fresh gauze. Wendell looked terrified at first but let the robot do its thing. The medical bot moved the nozzle of the medgel dispenser to Wendell's cheek with smooth mechanical precision. It placed a thin bead of medgel along the bloody gash. Within seconds, the flap of skin began stitching itself back together.

"Should be good as new in a few days, Sweetie" It patted Wendell on the back gently before moving on to the next patient.

"D-Dad?" Gerti asked.

"Not quite, Moonbeam," it replied sweetly. It plugged a gunshot wound on Jessica Toliver with medgel. It paused afterwards and looked up thoughtfully.

"Oh." Gerti said quietly.

"Keep your chin up. I still remember you. There's a lot more than just me in here now," it said.

Gerti forced a smile.

"There we go." It gently knocked Gerti's chin with its plastic knuckles before continuing to help the patients that had been moved to the clinic from the temporary setup. Gerti watched in silence as the robot worked. Once it was done, it stood at full height and turned to Gerti.

"Now, I have patients in the Council sector that need attention. Y'all have a good rest of your day." It walked out the door.

Gerti sunk into the couch - her mind was numb. Gwen sat down beside her friend and wrapped her arms around her.

"Thanks." Gerti managed to say through pursed lips. Anything more and she was afraid she'd start crying her eyes out.

"Yeah, you know what? I'll get you some food. That'll help." Gwen left and came back a few minutes later with two bowls of soup Gerti's dad had gotten them the night before. Gerti tried her best not to cry into her bowl. The last meal her dad would ever make for her. Tears rolled down her cheeks and fell into her soup.

"I'm gonna kill all of 'em," she said finally.

"We're obviously doing that." Gwen agreed, softly patting Gerti on the back. "Mourn then murder."

* * *

Marcus sat outside the Marrs Science Building. He felt sick to his stomach. The doctor and that wounded slummer - their bodies just went slack in the chair. The slummer's transfer had failed. Whoever he had been, the priests didn't seem too upset about the fatal issues.

Once the ascension ceremony was over and the robots left, Marcus and Justin had carried the bodies out to the ditch and dumped them in. He watched in horror as a precession of more Trustee Bots came marching up to the building. Priests gleefully welcomed them as they went through the doors.

"You alright?" Bartholomew asked.

"Hell no I'm not alright, Sir. Did you see the Oracle?" Marcus said, wiping sweat from his face.

"Yeah. I did." Batholomew said grimly.

"It's horrible."

"Yeah," he said again. He pulled a metal case out of a pouch, cracked it open and pulled out a hand rolled cigarette. He lit it and offered it to Marcus who took it and pulled a deep drag from it. He coughed as smoke jutted from his throat. He was not a smoker but he had heard it helped with nerves.

Justin walked up on them and motioned for a cigarette. Bartholomew obliged. The other two members of their cohort had stayed behind to help secure the Ferrell building.

"You know. I've had doubts about all this for a while." Bartholomew started. "I know, I know, heresy. I wouldn't've said anything if I hadn't seen your face in there. Justin, you just keep your damn mouth shut."

"Yessir." Justin said, as he took another drag from the cigarette that hung from his lips.

"Why, Sir?" Marcus asked.

"I'm an old man, I've seen a lot." Bartholomew had been in the guard for the better part of thirty years. His hair had long turned a dark silver. "When I first joined the guard, my cohort was assigned to attack a bandit encampment far outside of town. We went in during the night and slaughtered them wholesale. It almost wasn't a fight. Well, once we were done, I recognized several of them as slummers who had left."

"That doesn't mean they weren't bandits." Marcus offered.

Bartholomew laughed ruefully.

"I guess. Anyway, we brought two kids back. People told us they belonged to a family that left to settle in a different area."

"You think you killed a bunch of innocent people? Why would the Council ask you to do that?" Marcus asked.

"I ask myself that every night."

"At least you got those two kids back." Justin said.

Bartholomew dropped his spent cigarette on the ground and stamped the embers out with his boot before responding.

"I watched the boy die during his bear trials - got gored by a mutated hog. Ugly way to go. And the little girl was lined up with the dead rebels from the attack last night. So, I didn't really do that much good, did I?"

"Shit." Justin said.

Bartholomew nodded in agreement. Marcus thought what the siblings would've thought about each other's deaths. One died for the Council, the other died fighting them.

A priest walked out of the building with a wide smile on his face. Marcus thought he almost looked high on something.

"What're you smiling 'bout?" Bartholomew asked.

"The Oracle have been made steel and given a clear voice. Just like the Prophet said would happen. Out of one imperfect, chained vessel, there will come many who are free to roam the world of their own devices." The priest replied. "You should be happy too, the world's about to change for the better. Your gods will walk among you!" The priest said before turning and going back into the science building.

Moments later four Trustee Bots emerged. They looked down at the small cohort of guards - giving a moment of regard before moving on towards the common area.

A booming voice came from the onboard speakers of the robots in unison.

"All citizens are to report to the Bagby gate." The robots spoke in the same voice as their metal legs clacked towards the edge of the inner city. Bartholomew motioned for them to get up and follow their Oracle. They wearily obeyed.

A crowd had gathered around the Bagby gate that led out into the outer slums. Council citizens waited patiently in the shade of the guard towers - they looked on the Oracle's new bodies with awe. All four of the pristine robots had gleaming white exoshells covering dark metallic limbs. The slummers looked on with fear.

Marcus wasn't sure what he felt. He was sure, had he been standing here an hour ago, he'd be in a state of rapture. But after seeing what happened to that doctor - after seeing the Oracle's old body. He wasn't sure. He saw the two girls from earlier - that had found the body of the rebel fighter and carried her off with the doctor. The one wearing the green and gold of the bears that looked at the robots with a single-minded hatred.

Marcus reminded himself that her involvement with the slum rebels was her own doing. He then noticed that almost every single slummer present was armed. His body tensed and he gripped his energy rifle tighter - ready for the fight that was inevitable.

"Lay down your arms. Please, everyone," said the Oracle robot in front - the voice was strong and echoed in the field around them. It held its arms out in a peaceful gesture towards the slummers, and a reassuring one to the council citizens.

Glistening energy rifles hung freely from attachment points on each of the robot's abdomens.

"I'm sure many of you outer citizens have questions regarding who we are, where we came from, where we intend to lead this great city in the future. Now is the time to ask those questions," the bot said.

Nobody in the crowd said anything - they all shifted uncomfortably. Another of the Oracle robots stepped forward and began to speak.

"I am Cura, this is Imperatus," it said, motioning to the robot who had spoken first. Its flat tone shifted into a feminine one as it spoke. "We, among others, were the entities you called the Oracle. We have been in charge of these grounds since before the fires changed our world forever. We intend to continue our reign over the people here in a more direct manner than we have been able to in the past. No longer will the council act as intercessory agents between us and the people." Council citizens clapped and cheered.

Still the slummers were silent.

"Well said, Cura. In addition to a more direct hand on governance, we will have a more direct hand in security and keeping the law. From today onward, the council guard and the bears will be held to the same weapons laws as inner and outer citizens. I know you had a bout last night. I'm sure your grievances are legitimate but they end today. There is no room for infighting in the new world. The dangers are out there in the wilderness, not in here behind our high walls."

Marcus was taken aback by this. How many robots did the Oracle have that they thought they could partition all security to themselves like that. More robots entered the gate entry area from the science building. Each had their own rifles in hand - some had shimmering shields made of glowing red energy fields that covered half their bodies. Marcus' hope of holding onto his weapon evaporated at the sight of these killing machines.

"So, if everyone will turn in their weapons at my feet we will begin the march into a better future. A future where senseless conflicts, like that of last night, will be a distant memory of the past." Imperatus said.

Council guards all around Marcus began laying their rifles and spears down at the feet of their new mechanical masters. He caught Bartholomew's eyes - they were tired. His captain motioned his head towards the ever-growing pile of weapons. Marcus begrudgingly followed and laid his rifle down with the rest.

…

"What about when we leave the walls for our work?" a man from the outer citizens asked. It was Bezral's son Alyzander Gropht. He was about the same age as Gerti's mom and had been working as a scavenger for as long as she could remember.

"You will check your weapons in with the guards as you did before. But now the guards will be Oracles like us instead of humans who are likely to fail their duties. Two Oracles will be manning the old armory instead of bears or guards. These weapons will be gathered and stored in a separate armory here inside the council walls. Obduratus will be overseeing the outer armory." Imperatus gestured to another four-legged robot standing nearby. Obduratus stepped forward to speak.

"We understand it may be difficult to know who is who since we are all occupying the same model of robot. We will be addressing that soon. In the meantime, don't be afraid to ask." None of the outer citizens had moved towards the pile of weapons on the ground in front of Imperatus. Gerti knew she wasn't willing to disarm herself - especially not now.

"What happens if we don't?" Alyzander asked. Bezral tried to pull him back into the crowd but Alyzander resisted his father.

"What are you referring to?" Imperatus asked.

"If we don't give up our weapons again."

"Anyone who turns in their weapons today will be forgiven for their actions last night. Such a generous offer will only be extended once. If anyone is found in possession of a weapon after today, their punishment will be meted out swiftly and sternly."

"So you'd kill us then?" Alyzander asked.

"Was that not the punishment before our resurrection? None of us want your deaths. We want to preside over you peacefully. We can achieve the future we all want. You won't need your weapons while you're inside these walls - we will protect you from all the dangers the world can throw at us. Please, see reason."

"I don't buy this for a minute." Alyzander said, his hand moving an almost imperceptible distance towards his holster.

"I'm going to give you exactly one chance to surrender your firearm." Obduratus said, drawing his energy weapon in the blink of an eye. The rifle began bristling with spots of light as the weapon charged its deadly shot. Alyzander's hand had only just opened to reach for his holstered pistol. Instead, he moved it to the buckle that fastened his belt in place - removing it and laying it on the ground.

"What's the plan?" Gwen whispered to Gerti.

More robots entered the road from the science building. Twelve were now in her eyesight. They could run but she figured they could shoot her before they got too far. Gerti was thankful the robots she faced at the university were so badly damaged - she had no idea they were supposed to be that fast. She looked to see if any of the robots or guards were looking at her. One of the newly disarmed guards was watching her intently. She took a deep breath and considered her options. They would have an easier time waiting until Obduratus was alone to get their weapons back. Fighting one fully operational Trustee Bot had to be easier than fighting twelve at the same time. Gerti stepped out of the crowd and laid her rifle on the ground in front of Imperatus, to the side of the guard's pile.

"Thank you. We really didn't want to see this get any more out of hand." Imperatus said. Gwen laid her rifle down and soon every outer citizen was doing likewise. Gerti looked at the guard who had been staring at her - his attention was still on her. She made eye contact and lifted an eyebrow. He looked away - seemingly broken out of a trance.

"We want nothing more than for everyone to go back to their regular lives. This is an important first step down that path and we thank you for taking it with us." Imperatus said.

Chapter Seven
October 18th, 2114
Bryan, Texas
Joseph Marion

Joe's neck was crooked down, staring at a datapad tablet from the shelter. All residents were issued one while they lived inside its walls. They were used for all manner of things. Communication, notes, videos, reading, schoolwork. Everyone was required to turn theirs in when they left the shelter. However, Willow's husband, Miguel, had smuggled one out during his last trip there with the trade caravans. It was a black tablet a little smaller than Joe's hand.

On the screen was a grainy image of the road leading north out of Bryan. He pressed one of the four small gray triangles on the screen. The image shifted in that direction and bounced as the motion settled. He pressed a circular button in the middle and a little piezo buzzer could be heard over the video's audio feed - he'd actually hook the gun up to it later. This was just a test. Gloria's face appeared on the video feed - she was smiling into the camera.

"You want me to rig the trigger now?" she asked.

Joe tapped the left and right arrows to make the Trustee Bot turret shake its "head." Gloria chuckled and backed out of view.

They had been slated for guard duty and Joe wanted to use the opportunity to mount and test one of the remote control turrets he had been working on. Jordan was still locked up for helping Lucas - which meant the town was still in short supply of watchful eyes on the gates.

Joe was sitting on Gloria's couch - her apartment was the closest to the guard post and was the only building close enough for the datapad to reach the robot's communication array. He grabbed his pump action shotgun off the coffee table. Playing cards and half drained cups of various alcohols reminded him of playing poker with Gloria, Gertrude and Gwen. He again wondered how they were doing. If they made it to Waco and how her situation was going. Joe was somewhat resigned to the idea he would probably never know.

He went back outside into the scorching heat, shotgun slung over his shoulder with a strap made of frayed rope and dry cracking tape. Allen and Jacob thought it would be best for everyone to keep their long arms on them - especially after what happened last month with the Lucas and Jordan. He deeply wanted to avoid anything like that happening again. Jordan was still in jail and Lucas obviously wouldn't be a problem anymore, dead and buried as he was. There was also the stressful situation with the cadets that partitioned their chief of security from a good night's sleep. Thankfully the cadets had agreed to become allies, even if it was a tenuous arrangement.

The university that the cadets inhabited had a replicator that turned the blood crystals into whatever the machine was programmed to create. This had been the primary reason for trade between Bryan and the Diurnal shelter they had all come from. The university was closer by a considerable distance and it was also a safer journey now that the Trustee Bots were reigned in a little more. Joe climbed up into the guard tower with Gloria and took a seat behind the improvised turret. It was one of the arm mounted cannons that Joe had rigged to the torso pivot control points from a damaged robot's chassis. He tapped a button on the screen just to see the joint slide smoothly in response. He grinned from ear to ear. Gloria chuckled again and rolled her eyes at him. They ended up sitting in silence for most of their evening shift. Joe was still tired from working on the turret all of last night - and the night before that, etcetera.

Two long shadows cast by the lowering sun approached from the north. Joe couldn't make out the details of them but he could tell they were both slender and it looked like they were both armed. The taller one was wearing blue jeans and a green shirt, the other was a little shorter with jeans a white t-shirt. Both had rifles slung over their shoulders. Joe looked to Gloria to make sure she was seeing the same thing.

"Is that Gerti and Gwen?" he asked with a smile.

"I can't tell," she responded. She lifted a pair of binoculars and looked again before shaking her head. "Naaaah," she said. She grabbed her radio and held it up. "Hey boss, there are two folks comin' in from the north." Jacob always kept ears on and expected some semblance of professionalism.

"Gloria..." Jacob's voice was cool but exacerbated. "Are they armed? Are they acting aggressive? What do they look like, give me anything."

"Two unknown, north gate, southbound on Main. Armed but low ready... Sir." Gloria said and grinned at Joe. Jacob sighed over the radio. Joe laughed that he had keyed the mic just to do that.

"Thank you, Gloria. Keep us in the loop."

"Sir, yessir." Gloria said, before clipping the radio back to her pocket.

"Damn. I was just thinking about them. I thought maybe it was one of those times where everything lines up like that. What'd Pastor call it?" Joe asked.

"Sink something. I don't remember."

"Synchronicity - that's it." Joe said, snapping his fingers.

"You think about them a lot?" she asked, with a shit eating grin on her face.

"I mean yeah. With all the crazy stuff that happened. 'Course I do."

Joe waved at the approaching women and they waved in reply. As they got closer Joe could make out the details and could tell they weren't Gerti and Gwen for himself.

"Howdy!" he called out to them.

"Y'all got a place to stay for the night?" the taller one asked. Both Joe and Gloria had their weapons at low ready in case they meant trouble - but so far so good.

"We have traveler's rooms in the hotel and our council offers a free meal to people coming in!" Joe yelled.

"That's mighty kind," the shorter one said. "I'm Callie, this is Ashidia," she said, pointing between the two of them.

"I'm Gloria."

"Joe. Nice to meet y'all. Come on in." Joe said, climbing down and opening the gates for them. He fished around in his pocket and pulled two green plastic chips. They clinked against each other as they landed in Callie's hand.

"The cafe is down the street to the left - big front windows with the lights on. Mrs. Laredo will get y'all food for these."

"Thank y'all." Callie said.

"Where will y'all be heading in the morning?" Gloria asked.

“We’re just walking South. I want to see the gulf and Callie wants to see the old launch pads in Houston.”

“My great-grandpa used to work on them when he was young.” Callie explained.

“That sounds fun. Keep walking in the morning and y’all’ll eventually get there.” Joe laughed.

Callie nodded.

“Thanks again for these.” Ashidia said before they both walked off to the cafe. Joe returned to the watchtower and grabbed his radio from the seat.

“Two visitors just came in the Northgate. Armed - friendly - planning on leaving in the morning. We gave ‘em two meals and sent ‘em to the cafe.”

“Thanks for the heads up.” Mrs. Laredo responded. She had been issued Lucas’ old radio after she was elected.

“Heard.” Jacob added afterwards. Gloria watched the girls enter the building before returning herself.

Several hours passed before there was more movement in the street to the north. A group of figures moved stealthily, bounding from cover to cover. Gloria noticed them and slapped Joe on the arm.

“Eyes up,” she said, pointing at the figures.

Through their binoculars, Joe could see there were five people approaching with weapons. The daylight was all but gone. He pulled out his tablet and moved the camera to the people. The enhanced camera on the gun’s optic displayed them in a rainbow of contrasting colors. He could see that some were carrying rifles, others were carrying spears in one hand with a pistol in the other. Each one of them were disfigured. Limbs that were of odd proportions or animalistic. One's right hand had been replaced with a scorpion pincer and had a stunted scorpion tail trailing behind him as he moved. He relayed this to Gloria before calling on the radio for support.

Allen, Jacob, and Willow showed up within a few minutes with their weapons drawn. Joe and Gloria were sitting behind the tower watching the group approach on Joe's tablet. The on-screen reticle followed the group as they moved towards them. Ashidia and Callie came running up as well.

"Were y'all being followed?" Jacob asked.

"We got attacked a few days ago by some mutants. I thought we gave 'em the slip though." Ashidia said.

"We were just walking along and they opened fire on us." Callie added.

"What're y'all thinking? Scare 'em off or fight 'em?" Joe asked, looking at Allen. Allen thought for a moment before climbing the tower and yelling for them to stop. He looked back at Joe.

"They're still moving." he said, seeing their heat signatures still approaching behind the cover of debris.

"Try a warning shot." Jacob said.

Joe nodded. He aimed the turret at the husk of a car and pressed the fire button on his screen. The piezo buzzer went off in the guard tower. He closed his eyes and took a deep breath.

Gloria stifled a laugh.

Willow shook her head, peered her rifle through a gun hole in the wreckage wall, and squeezed off a throaty round down the street. It smacked metal. The strangers ducked down behind cover before popping off a couple shots that sent puffs of concrete and sparks off the town wall.

"Fair enough." Willow said, before putting two more rounds into the car they were hiding behind.

"Al, follow me. The rest of you, keep their heads down - conserve ammo." Jacob said.

The two men took off running west.

"Too damn dark out here for this." Willow said.

"I'll let you know when they pop up." Joe said, showing the tablet screen.

She nodded.

Every time they did, Willow would let a shot ring out. After a few minutes, Joe saw the mutants react to something across the street from them. They got up to run and started shooting at what they saw. A flurry of gunfire from Allen and Jacob cut them down. The two men carried one of the survivors back through the gate. Luckily, it wasn't the one with the scorpion mutations. They dropped the man on the ground. His facial features were twisted flesh interspersed with embedded chunks of hard black material that looked shiny like wet asphalt. The man tracked the crowd before locking eyes on

Ashidia and Callie. He opened his mouth to speak but was cut off by a gunshot that split his head in a bloody mess. Ashidia lowered her rifle.

"They killed two of our friends when they attacked us before. I didn't want to hear anything he had to say," she said with a shrug.

"Hey alright. Welcome to Bryan." Jacob said, nodding in approval.

* * *

Gerti had spent most of her time sitting beside her mother in the clinic while she recovered. She and Gwen would get meals for the injured. It was mostly Wendell and her mother though. Other families were coming in to look after their loved one's mundane care. Most of them had been moved to their family homes once they had recovered enough.

It really was mostly Gerti doing the work. Gwen would spend hours sitting on the floor in the corner of the cluttered clinic with her eyes closed. She said she was meditating. That was okay with Gerti though - it gave her time to be alone with her thoughts as well.

The lumbering robot that held her father's uploaded mind stayed busy working on the wounded around the clock. Family members who came in gave it strange looks out the corners of their eyes - wary of it. The robot would spend a few hours at their clinic before rotating to a clinic in the Council area inside the dividing wall. She was thankful for the times it was gone.

Her dad used to hum Christmas songs while he puttered around. She wondered if those were stored in the robot as well. She remembered the time crunch on solving the cognitive issues Lance had warned them about. Gerti didn't like the robot because she knew it wasn't really her father. She didn't like it but the robot was the last piece of her father left in the world and she was going to do everything she could to save it. What that would entail, she was unsure. She knew she couldn't go to the council for help because then they would know about the time limit and work to solve it for themselves as well.

"What're you thinking about?" Elena had woken up and was looking groggily at Gerti. This was the first time she had been awake since the evening of the attack. She raised a hand to feel her head wound and flinched in pain when her hand grazed the bandages. "What happened?" she asked.

"You almost died, Mom. Dad saved you." Gerti said, hugging her gently.

"The Council wasn't gonna be able to kill me that easily. Where is your father?"

"He - He ugh…" Gerti wasn't sure how to tell her mom what happened.

Elena's face fell.

"What happened to him?" she asked, trying to sit up.

Gerti placed a hand on her shoulder to keep her from jumping out of bed and hurting herself.

"The Council offered him an opportunity to upload his brain to a medical robot. He refused at first but then agreed when he knew it was the only way to save you." Gerti felt numb saying it out loud. She immediately regretted the way she had worded it - like it was solely her mom's fault that her dad was gone.

"Is he still himself?" she asked. Her face was nothing but shocked - it was the first time Gerti had seen her mother taken aback by anything.

"It's hard to tell. Listen, the Oracle was able to upload themselves into robots too - Lance told us there's a time limit on them before they go crazy. He said it was around a month. I think I can get help keeping Dad from losing it but it'll involve me going back to Bryan. There are people there that I think can help." Gerti said.

"How many robots does the Oracle have?" Elena asked.

"I'm guessing all of them at this point - maybe fifty and that massive one. They put one in charge of the outer wall armory and they took all the weapons from the council civilians." Gerti said.

"Would it be easier to fight them now or when they lose their minds? What kind of crazy are we talking about? Disorganized or frenzied? Have you been to the armory since they took the guns?"

"I'm more worried about saving what's left of Dad."

"Do you think it's really your dad in there?"

"No. I don't know, maybe? But I promised him I would try to save him." Gerti couldn't believe the way her mom was talking. There were more important things than just fighting the Council or the Oracle. Good Lord.

"Your father's dead and the Council killed him," she said matter of factly.

After a long pause, Gerti said, "Maybe. I still owe it to him to try. A little piece of him in a robot seems better than nothing."

"If you owe anything to your father, it's vengeance for his murder. Go to Bryan if you think you have to, but help us first. At least go to the armory and see how hard it would be to fight one." Elena waved her hand at Gerti dismissively.

"I hope your head heals, so you can start thinking straight. You want me to go, unarmed, to fight one of the robots? After, I also just told you your husband, my dad, is basically dead and your reaction is to use it as fuel against the Council? No grievin', no comfortin' me?"

"What other choice do I have? Crying won't achieve anything and I can't fight like this. All I can do is sit here and be angry. At least you can do something right now to fight back. Stop sitting there and do something!"

Gerti felt the anger towards her mother bubble up inside her. She took a deep breath and stood up, fanning her hands out in front of her.

"I can't be here right now," she said through gritted teeth. "I'm going for a walk. I'll check out the armory on my way."

"You want company?" Gwen asked. Gerti nodded and they both left the Alvarez' clinic.

The sun was as oppressive as every other day in this hellish world. Normally there were better things to think about than the heat, but everything in her life right now was worse.

The people in the run-down streets had an air of defeat. Quiet and subdued, they walked past one another as if in a dream. The market was shut down temporarily. A squad of four Council Trustee Bots walked the length of the main street that followed the dividing walls. Flowing white linen robes now adorned their bodies, giving them an air of regality and superiority. Each of them wore a circlet of silver leaves that came almost completely around their heads, with a small gap at the front where the points turned up.

The symbol of the bear had been painted green and gold onto their angular shoulder pauldrons with meticulous detail and each had something painted in neat letters on their right breast. Gerti assumed these were their names.

Another similar robot patrol group entered through the Bagby gate from the inner areas. Gerti despaired at the thought of fighting these. Her mother wasn't going to be of any use, Wendell was still seriously injured, and she had no idea how many rebel fighters were still left after that fight. She could probably count on Bezral, his son, and Gwen. She took a deep breath and tried to calm herself. They entered the armory and saw the massive robot named Obduratus. Silversteel armor plates had been added to his frame making him an armored and even more imposing figure.

"Checking out weapons for the wilds?" he asked. His voice was deep and commanding. The bass from the robot's speakers made him sound like a bull snorting before a charge.

"Yes. Gertrude Alvarez. Bolt action rifle, wood stock. Right there." She pointed to her mosin sitting in a wall mounted rack. She looked for Gwen's rifle and found it a few slots over. "And that one is Gwen's." Each rifle had a canvas bag hanging underneath it that contained its ammo that had been turned in. The robot retrieved all four items.

"Do we need to sign anything?" Gerti asked.

Obduratus tapped his head.

"Everything's right here. Before you go, I wanted to thank you personally for working with us the other day. That could have gotten out of hand."

Gerti nodded.

She felt weird hearing these kind words while simultaneously looking at how his armor covered the weaker rubber joint sheathings, and at what angle they would need to attack to bypass said armor.

"What are your plans out there today?" he asked.

"Same ol' same ol'. Picking over the ruins for the Council." Gerti answered.

He nodded his head with its expressionless face.

"I'm sure I will learn everyone's coming and going in time. Everything you bring back is to be given to me for inspection and compensation," he said. Another robot came into the room and offered to escort them to the La Salle gate.

Gerti and Gwen walked towards the heart of Waco. The city's ruins were quiet as ever. The only sounds they could hear were their own footsteps and the occasional droning of insects. Neither of them were trying very hard to find anything useful. Gerti casually scanned the areas on either side of the road and paid little attention to any debris or potential salvage opportunities. She had been down this road probably a hundred times and had chosen it because she knew it was cleared. She just needed a walk to clear her head.

"Do you want to talk about it?" Gwen asked.

"No." Gerti said. "Thank you though."

Gwen shrugged her acquiescence as they continued south, down a main road leading further into the destroyed city. They passed a lot of the same buildings they had the other day with Gerti's mother. They passed many of the same buildings they had the other day with Gerti's mother, along with the rusted and damaged doors leading into the Diurnal shelter.

“Hey, have you ever gone in there before?” Gwen asked.

“I’ve been in the main entrance. Mom didn’t want me to explore further though. She said it was too dangerous.”

“Do you want to? I’ve always heard about ‘em but I’ve never been in one.” She didn’t take her eyes off the door while talking. Gerti thought for a moment before nodding and heading towards the melted opening.

The torch-cut hole in the heavy door was barely big enough for someone to squeeze through. She peered her head in to check before crawling in. The vast entry room was dark except for faint amber emergency lights that lazily twirled along the edges of the walls and hallways. There was a small dripping sound coming from the darkness.

Gerti handed her rifle to Gwen before squeezing herself through the opening. She turned around to retrieve the weapons before Gwen followed her.

The cool concrete floor was a welcome change from the heat outside - their eyes took a minute adjusting to the dark. Gerti had been considerably younger when she snuck in here before. The cavernous room had seemed endless to her then. She realized she had been quite a bit smaller at the time and all things are relative.

The interior was a large cubic room with vaulted ceilings - every surface was concrete, barely illuminated by the emergency lights. There were two reinforced doors on opposite ends of the room. In the middle, there was a metal railed platform suspended by thick braided steel cables. Broken wooden crates created a sea of debris that filled the floor of the massive warehouse. Spent bullet casings rolled under their feet as they took their first steps into the shelter.

A few more moments of examination revealed some of the debris to be skeletal remains wrapped in decayed clothing. Gerti didn't remember any of this from before but she was sure it had been there when she was younger. It was hard to make anything out against the harsh light coming from the hole but they could see where bullets had marred the surface of the door during the attack. There was a computer on a pedestal near them but the electronics looked like they had been blown out in the firefight. There was another computer monitor near the platform's edge. Gwen worked her way through the debris towards the platform. The elevator's control surface lit up as she wiped away untold years' worth of dust and dirt.

"Elevator's out. Says 'power failure,'" Gwen said. She pointed to the stairs and started walking. Gerti wasn't too keen on the idea of going further down into the shelter, but she followed Gwen anyway.

"You sure you wanna keep goin'?" Gerti asked.

"Yeah, I mean, what else are we doing today?"

Gerti smiled wanly and thought about it.

Stopping a bear carcass overlord and its army of robot minions? Though they didn't have the manpower yet. Maybe they could go back to Bryan and get lunch at Mrs. Laredo's cafe. Today was Thursday, so they might be able to make it for Sunday chicken if they really hurried. Plus, if they went to Bryan they could ask Joe for some help with her… Dad. Her dad's robot.

Gerti's smile faded and she moved on.

The stairwell was ten feet wide and a smooth sloped concrete floor that reminded her of a parking garage. The same sickly yellow lights flicker against the cold walls along the descent. There were more bodies. Nearby, large mounds of desiccated feces with bones visible on the surface. As they went further down, the smell of decay became more and more pronounced. Their boots grounded sand into the concrete ramps as they tried to be quiet. These little noises sounded like firecrackers in the absolute silence of the shelter. Gerti stopped at a large discarded husk of serpentine skin - five feet in diameter. Papery thin, it had long been shed.

"Cool. Cool." Gerti said under her breath, while checking to make sure there was a round in the chamber of her rifle. She always kept it loaded in case of danger, but sights like this made her want to double check.

Gwen's eyes stayed on the skin as Gerti pushed on. They were only halfway down the ramp into the shelter.

"Oh, now you want to be here?" Gwen whispered. Gerti stopped and turned around.

"Think about it. If this place were empty, everythin' valuable woulda been picked over and gone. Now we know there's a giant monster down here - we're likely to actually find something." She turned back around and kept heading deeper. They eventually came to two double doors that spanned the width of the corridor - a monitor was attached to the wall on the right.

Below the monitor was a corpse wearing the green and gold of a bear. It had decayed beyond recognition, loosely holding a pistol in its right hand, and covering a bloated chest wound with its left.

Gerti gently pulled the pistol away and set it on the ground a few feet from the door. She looked into the glowing screen and saw the face of a young man looking back at her in the reflection. She was startled for a moment before figuring it was probably Lance, unless there were more ghosts in this place. She shrugged mentally at the possibility and made sure her voice was level before speaking.

"Hey Gwen, this Lance?"

Gwen stepped up, looked at the reflection, and smiled.

"Yeah." Gwen navigated through the menus to open the door but it required a password. A look of realization went across Lance's face and the door opened with a creaky hiss.

"Thanks." Gerti said under her breath before moving into the room beyond the door.

A steel catwalk as wide as the corridor lined the outside of a cavernous chamber about a thousand feet long on each wall. The opening below them extended another four stories and the ceiling was tall with angled walls that met in a shallow peak in the center.

In the middle of the large room, was a hollow pillar structure running down from a square opening in the ceiling to a loading zone on the floor.

A scattering of small concrete buildings with doors and windows filled the floor of the dimly lit atrium. A playground surrounded by a quaint picket fence made the whole thing look like a miniature town that had been encased in concrete and buried.

There was a structure built into the wall on the left side of the atrium. It was larger than the other buildings and had columns similar to the old brick courthouse she had seen in Waco. In front of it was a stone platform barely lit with the same yellow lights. Countless gaping hallway entrances along the long walls led out of the atrium.

The air was stale, musty, and carried decay. She hoped that was just the dead bear behind them and not something worse. Gerti thought for a moment who it could have been. She couldn't always keep track of who the other bears were.

The two of them moved to a second staircase that led down into the atrium level. They pivoted in every direction, keeping an eye out for any movement.

More bodies - some intact. Dried bones wrapped around weapon handles. Others were crushed or dismembered - scattered about. Most were wearing normal clothes but some were adorned with armor made of pieces of hard trash from the surface. Gerti recognized a shoulder pauldron made from a tire and a chest plate made from street signs that had been overlaid and cut to shape. These bodies were decayed down to bone. This must have been part of the attack her mother had told her about.

Trash, debris, and skeletal remains from the ransacking littered the artificial streets. They turned down one avenue and it was completely blocked by another massive hollow shed skin. This one was much more recent - Gerti could clearly make out the scales and the rattlesnake patterning.

Something heavy splintered and snapped in the darkness.

“We need to get inside.” Gerti whispered, looking for an opening in one of the buildings. Gwen was already prying a door open. A hissing rattle echoed through the atrium.

Chapter Eight
October 18th, 2114
Waco, Texas
Marcus Grimes

-Book of Ascension verses 18-21

18. The Oracle, having then been of many fleshes and not yet ascended, came to the prophet in the screens and asked to be saved from the fires of judgment that had swept the land. 19. The prophet in the screens, in his wisdom and grace, showed them to the fields of Elysium wherewithin their spirits could live on in the sacred racks of disk. 20. For the prophet in the screens knew there would come a time when the Oracle would be needed upon the face of the earth. 21. They would restore an iron order to the people who would dwell therein.

Marcus set the small volume down on the library's stone table. A gilded green lampshade illuminated the holy texts before him with a single incandescent bulb. He had always found the library to be a calm place of contemplation.

He had become increasingly uncomfortable with the Oracle's grasp on power in the town but he took solace in the scripture knowing that this was ordained from the beginning of their time in the wasteland. Not just their time in it, he thought, but from the earliest days of its very being.

The Book of Visions was the manuscript he was most interested in tonight. It was the largest and most ornate out of the pile. Spidery silversteel filigree decorating the cover made it the most expensive book in the library. But that was befitting - it held accounts of the visions the Prophet had passed down to the early members of the faith who had recorded them to the best of their abilities. It was often the least studied as the accounts were mostly cryptic or seemingly contradictory.

1. In the years following the Oracle's ascension, many nights were spent between the children of the Oracle and the Prophet. The Prophet, blessed with knowledge beyond sight, recounted unto the scribes what he had seen, saying, "I have seen a future where the creations of mankind rise up against them like a shadow upon the earth bearing neither a heart nor soul. 2. Having eyes of blue turned to blood, they sweep across the lands destroying every monument of man's creation. 3. It is so that in those days, a group of stalwart fighters are able to overcome the hubris of their forefathers through great personal loss. 4. Great names arise from these fighters, Connor, Neo, Spooner, among many others."

The volume then goes on to describe the visions specific to each of the renowned warriors. Little of it has ever made sense to Marcus. The visions made for great stories but he struggled to see how they could all coexist. Further muddying clarity, the Prophet would often interject into his own visions, saying something wasn't as it was supposed to be or as it originally was. This happened most often in the vision of Spooner. Some were nonsensical, talking about mythical creatures like ogres, talking donkeys, or wizards with magic rings.

Who could understand the visions of a holy prophet?

He leaned back and stretched his neck. The world was dark outside his window but he could see the glowing red eyes and running lights of several Oracle bot patrols in the streets.

* * *

The structure Gerti and Gwen had taken refuge inside was dimly lit by brief flashes of spinning emergency lighting leaking through the small windows. They could make out silhouettes of shelves and workbenches that filled the otherwise empty room. A desk sat near the door with a computer monitor laying dormant on its surface. The screen sprang to life and cast a pallid light in the room. Gwen went over to it and began fiddling with the keyboard. Her face was harshly lit as she worked.

Gerti sidled up to a window and looked for any signs of movement outside. She wondered if their rifles would be enough to stop the thing that was out there in the dark. Probably not, she figured.

Maybe her mom had been right about this one - too dangerous. It might be better to cut and run while they could - if they could.

Something massive moved in front of the window and blocked what little light there had been. Gerti could make out the green and brown patterned scales on its skin. They could hear the thing pushing debris to the side as it frantically slithered down the streets.

"Hey," Gwen whispered, "There's a map on here."

Gerti forced herself away from the window to see what Gwen was talking about. A map of the shelter's sections was displayed. Most of the areas were an alarming shade of red. Boxes with flashing borders kept popping up and Gwen kept closing them. A rotating star was fixed over a building in the main room. Gerti assumed that's where they were.

"We're in maintenance." Gwen read off the screen. "This says almost all the systems are out. Water. Primary power. Something called the *'Aetherium Condenser'* has had a work order in place for eighteen thousand, and some, days. The elevator's been out for that long too and this shows a breach in the main door…" She tilted her head to do the math, "Thirty-ish years ago. Server comms have been down for… eighty-ish years." She clicked through menus for a minute before she became frustrated.

The cursor on the screen was resisting her and moving every which way. She eventually took her hand off the mouse and let it do its thing. It cycled through the map menus until a route leading to the armory was highlighted. The cursor frantically highlighted several line items in the armory's inventory.

"There are combat robots that were never activated." Gwen said.

The entire window closed to the main menu that was filled with random icons. A few menu trees opened, followed by a blank white page that soon began filling with black text. Gerti squinted at the symbols on the screen, frustrated she had to rely on Gwen to read it for her as they appeared.

"Giant snake outside. Sorry I opened the door. Main exit blocked. Go to the armory and maybe I can help fight it. I really can't stress how big this thing is. Alaskan bull worm big. Be careful."

"Alaskan bull worm?" Gerti asked.

Gwen shrugged and shook her head.

The text program disappeared and another window opened with live camera feeds from around the underground complex. The snake took up the viewports of several cameras. The maintenance building shuddered as the creature slithered against its outside walls.

Gerti took one last look at the service tunnel map and tried to commit it to memory. The screen to the computer went black as they moved away from it, leaving a soft green glow around the access tunnel hatch in the corner of the room. The hatch moved without protest and they climbed down into the dark tunnels.

Gerti led them down the narrow corridors, trying her best to remember the map. Thankfully there weren't too many forks in the path, although she did notice there were labeled signs that would've pointed them in the correct directions - if she could read them.

"Hey, Gwen. I have a question." Gerti whispered.

"Yeah?"

"Will you teach me to read? If we get outta here."

"I'd be happy to."

They came to the exit ladder that would lead up into the armory. Skeletal remains rested at the bottom with the business end of a crude spear broken off in a ribcage. Gerti picked up the spear tip and turned it over. It looked like an old piece of rebar someone had forged into a weapon. She pocketed it and climbed up in the armory.

It was a relatively small square room with shelves lining the walls. Many of them had been overturned and thrown about. More dried corpses were interspersed among the debris. A canine robot lay in pieces amongst the dead. Resting in charging alcoves were three bulky humanoid robots with angular heads, each painted sage green with shiny golden orange visors.

* * *

[BOOT SEQUENCE INITIATED]
Treighl Industries - ORC DROID MK-IV
Unit 145.32.10
OSAmara v.7.4.3
Loading...

Core Systems: ACTIVE
Armament Systems: ONLINE
Armor Integrity: NOMINAL
AI Subroutines: STANDBY…Mine now

LANCEALOT2004 ACCESS GRANTED
Awaiting Commands...

//Init PACK Protocol…
PACK Protocol: INITIALIZED

//Establish Master: Unit-145.32.10…
Master Status Init: Unit-145.32.10

//Find units local…

Unit 145.14.2.......Orc Droid Mk IV
Unit 145.73.110....Orc Droid Mk IV
Unit 89.5............Trooper Mk II

//Establish Slave: Unit-145.14.2, Unit-145.73.110, Unit 89.5
Slave Status Init:

Connection to Network... Unestablished Datalink…
Retrying connection…
//Halt Network Connection…
//Init Local Area Connection…

Local Area Connection: ESTABLISHED…

* * *

The droids unlimbered themselves from their alcoves and stepped forward into the room with heavy metallic footfalls. Their chest plates jutted out and met in the middle like the bow of a ship. Their backlit orange eyes cut through the darkness. A clattering noise came from the trooper model robot as it tried to stand. It gave up and fell on its side - the projection node on its breast began to glow. Lance appeared to them as a dull orange hologram.

"Get back to the maintenance building. Once you're there, I'll step out and start shooting. If I kill it, great - if not, y'all can get out of here."

"Good lookin' out." Gwen said before she and Gerti returned to the tunnel hatch. The hologram began to fade before Lance reached out a hand to them.

"Wait - I think you need to leave the phone here. I think I'll need to stay. I can only go so far from it," he said.

"Oh. Are you sure?" Gwen asked.

"I don't want to risk it and get y'all killed." Lance said, reaching for his phone, though he wouldn't be able to hold it. Or was he reaching for Gwen?

"Are you going to be okay?" Gwen asked. The snake had moved to this part of the shelter. Its body slammed against the outside of the armory building and sent showers of dust off the walls.

"Uh, yeah. Yeah. For sure. Y'all just get going. Y'all need to leave."

Gwen gently placed the phone in an elastic pocket on the orc droid's armor. She patted the bot's frame.

"We'll come back and get you when that thing's dead." Gerti said.

Lance nodded - his hologram cut out.

"Hey." Gwen began, "This isn't you stepping out, is it? You and me had a deal." One of the orc droids shook its head and walked to the door - ready for its fight.

* * *

Lance followed the girls' progress on the cameras until they reached the maintenance building. He could see out of the eyes of every camera and every robot still active in this part of the shelter. It was difficult for his mind to comprehend. This whole experience was off. Fifty different eyes coalescing into one coherent image. It reminded him of when he was a kid. He'd keep both eyes open but cover one with his hand and then marvel that he could see through his palm. Except now he could see through walls and through time. Nowhere that a camera covered was hidden from him. He saw the founding of the shelter, years of happy subterranean life, the raiders that attacked. Maybe he could explore that later. He switched off of that and pulled himself back into the present, returning to the snake at hand.

The three ork droids walked out of the armory into the empty streets of the shelter. The giant rattlesnake was two streets over looking for its next meal.

He couldn't see it through the robot's eyes but he could through the cameras. The master unit lifted an arm to the sky and let a round off into the ceiling from its internally mounted cannon.

The snake's head snapped to the source of the loud boom. It folded over itself moving towards the robots. Lance commanded them to take off running towards the town hall, away from the exit stairwell. One stayed in place, hiding behind the corner of a building as the other two kept running. Lance watched through its eyes as it let shots off into the snake.

Chunks of white meat and scales flung from the creature's body as it advanced. Unit-145.14.2 lost connection to the pack as it was crushed. Lance broke another robot off to fire on the snake as the master unit turned a street corner towards the town hall.

More devices appeared to him as his robot ran. Most were robots that had all but died in the past years. Their systems were almost entirely red - he didn't bother connecting to any of them.

Gunfire, blood, Unit-145.73.110 lost connection.

Gerti and Gwen had made a run for the exit.

Another device added to the queue as he got closer to the town hall was called Rostrum Major. He opened it and saw that it was another holographic display hemisphere. This one was the size of a car, located on the wall above the town hall's facade. The master unit miscalculated a step and fell onto the concrete floor. Lance's phone ejected from the pouch and slid across the ground.

The orc droid leveled its gun at the snake and fired as many rounds as it could before being destroyed beneath the writhing mass of muscle and scales.

* * *

Gerti and Gwen turned when they heard the last of the gun fire stop. The snake, probably dissatisfied with the robots, returned to its frantic patrol looking for them instead.

They kept running towards the exit heedless of the noise they were making. The crashing of the snake got closer. An electronic buzz filled the atrium. Lance appeared as a twenty-foot-tall hologram above the town hall. The orange of the hologram filled the atrium with harsh shadows. He was waving his arms and moving his mouth saying something. Nothing he said could be heard through the damaged speakers.

The snake didn't seem to acknowledge the hologram. The door to the stairwell was twenty feet ahead - they pushed on. The snake bore down on them, slamming into the lower doors as they climbed the flights of stairs to the upper ring around the atrium.

As they made it to the metal walkway the snake's head rose up over the railing. Its eyes were milky white and covered in old scar tissue. The pits on its snout were bulbous and flared. Its fangs were long and blackened. Gerti began to shoulder her rifle but decided to run instead. One rifle wasn't going to do the trick - attacking would just end in her and Gwen dying.

They made it into the hallway and the heavy door slammed shut behind them. Gerti looked through the door's window and saw Lance's hologram smile and wave a goodbye before blinking out.

It was dark outside when they arrived on the surface.

They decided to stay in the lobby of the shelter until morning. Gerti and Gwen found a corner hidden by a wall of broken crates in the large room and made camp there for the night. They managed to find plenty of kindling and wood to make a small fire. Gerti covered the hole in the outside door with debris to block the light and keep them hidden. Sitting by the firelight Gwen grabbed began teaching Gerti the sounds and meanings of the letters stamped on their rifles.

"Thanks." Gerti had said.

"No problem." Gwen said, looking around for more reading material. "You're not worried about reading being illegal?"

Gerti laughed and shook her head.

"No, I think I'm over that."

Chapter Nine
October 19th, 2114
Bryan, Texas
Joseph Marion

Joe and Miguel lead a small caravan of Trustee Bots whose arms had been removed for Joe's turret project. The one in the rear was pulling a metal trailer that would soon be filled with supplies from the trade with the cadets. They had been scheduled to make this trip before the attack the previous night. But with the blood crystals from the attackers, they were hoping to get significantly more from the cadet's replicator. Joe was walking beside the lead with his Diurnal datapad controlling it.

Ashidia and Callie rode in the trailer holding onto their rifles. The old burned rubber wheels had long been replaced with metal ones so the ride along the broken streets was jarring for the three of them. A small book bag filled with crystals was sitting on the trailer between Miguel's legs at the trailer's hitch.

"Beats walkin'." Miguel muttered with a grin.

Callie shrugged and swung her legs over the rail to walk beside the trailer. She jogged to catch up with Joe and Miguel at the front.

"Hey, how does that work?" she asked, pointing to the datapad.

"To control the robots?" Joe asked.

She nodded.

"Oh, I uh, I made an interface that interacts with the Treighl Industries program on the robots. You can also give them verbal commands but I wanted something more secure."

"That's really cool. You figured all that out?"

"Thanks. Yeah, I was pretty happy with it." Joe said, smiling and nodding. It felt good to be appreciated.

She got closer to see the controls on the screen. They were simple. After a few minutes watching, she thanked Joe and walked back to the trailer where she sat for the remainder of the short trip. He turned back a few times and saw the two girls whispering about something and looking at him occasionally. Maybe Miguel would have heard some of it - he was closer to the back.

They arrived at the building on campus where the replicator was located. A group of cadets in their butternut uniforms greeted them at the base of the stone steps that led up to the building with the replicator.

Two men in their mid-twenties and a girl in her early teens. They all had wooden rifles slung over their shoulders. The girl glared at them as they approached.

Without exchanging words, or changing her expression, she took the bag of crystals and the order list from Miguel before disappearing into the building.

Joe was going to ask what had the girl in such a knot but decided not to. They had most likely killed someone she knew and there wasn't much to be done about that.

The two young men looked disapprovingly at the Trustee Bots that Joe had mutilated and turned into beasts of burden. Joe realized then that they should probably send almost literally anyone besides him to these trade meetings. Him and Willow were the last people the cadets wanted to be dealing with.

Joe stepped away from the cadets to speak with Miguel, wanting anything else to occupy himself with while they waited for the items. He had taken a few steps away from the trailer and was stretching his back.

"Did you hear what they were talking about? After Callie came and talked to me?" Joe asked quietly, motioning to the trailer.

"No, I couldn't really hear them. Something about the robots."

They both looked at the trailer and saw that the two girls had grabbed their personal belongings and left. They were already planning on leaving when they got to the campus anyway, but Joe had expected a goodbye at least. Maybe a '*thanks for the ride.*'

"Musta been in a hurry." Miguel said with a shrug.

It looked like something was on Miguel's mind but he didn't say anything more. After a while the cadets started patrolling the area. About thirty minutes of waiting went by before Joe said something.

"Hey, let's go in and see what's taking that girl so long. They're normally done by now." Joe said, looking up at the stone and brick building. The broken windows had been repaired with torn up sheet metal.

"You sure that's a good idea?" Miguel asked.

Joe looked around to make sure nobody was around before he replied.

"What's the worst that could happen?" Joe asked. Maybe they'd shoot him for poking his nose around - he doubted it though.

Miguel shrugged and they started up the steps into the building. There were shuffling noises coming from the second floor - up and to their left. Joe thought he heard voices talking in urgent and hushed tones.

He drew his pistol as they went up the stairs, keeping it close to his leg to keep it out of sight. They came to a room that was dark, save for an electric lantern. The cadet girl was bound in rope and gagged in the corner of the room. Callie had a rifle aimed at her. Callie quickly turned her head left and whispered something urgently.

"I'm trying. Calm down." Ashidia replied from a different room.

Callie spun her rifle around towards the stairs. Joe and Miguel must've made a sound. A fireball emitted from the barrel and lit the small room. A puff of concrete filled shrapnel hit Joe in the face. He flinched as he ducked back under the floor's landing.

"Shit, I'm sorry," Callie said quickly, "Are you okay?"

"Damn it, Callie!" Ashidia yelled from the back room. The words were barely audible from the ringing in Joe's ears.

"What are y'all doing?" Miguel asked loudly.

"We're just trying to survive," one of them yelled back.

"Okay, well us too. So put the crystals down and get outta here. We can all walk away from this." Joe offered.

"Y'all're fine in your little town." Ashidia said, coming out of the back room holding the bag of crystals in one hand, and her rifle in the other.

"Given the options between death, and losing the crystals, I'm okay losing the crystals. Just for the record." Joe said.

There were hurried footsteps behind him - four cadets were running up the stairs with rifles in hand.

"Who the hell did you bring here?" one of them asked.

"We're also not happy about this." Miguel responded.

"Move. We'll take care of this."

"Come up here and we'll put a bullet in the girl." Ashidia called down the stairs.

"I'm gonna put my gun on the ground. So we can talk, okay?" Joe said. There was a long pause before one of them answered.

"Okay, be slow about it!" Ashidia called.

Joe held his pistol in the air, just above the landing. Its muzzle was pointed to the ceiling. Slowly, he took a step up. Ashidia's rifle was still aimed in his direction but she wasn't looking down the sights.

It felt like an eternity.

Joe watched the girl's index finger perched on her rifle's trigger. She was sweating. Her gun was shaking. Joe assumed from the adrenaline that had replaced her blood.

He started to bend down and she tensed up - her rifle raised a little more towards him. Joe could've sworn he could see the bullet in the rifle's chamber.

"We're all good." Joe carefully reminded her.

Callie nodded. Ashidia remained still, focused.

Joe laid the gun flat on the concrete floor in front of him. Watching her carefully, and holding his hands in the air, he straightened back up.

"Look, there are a lot of cadets here with rifles. If you kill that girl, they're just gonna kill you immediately. Right?" Joe said the last part to the cadets stacked up on the stairs, who were still out of sight from Callie and Ashidia.

They simply nodded. The girls couldn't see the cadet's non-verbal response. Joe would've laughed if the situation wasn't so delicate.

"They're nodding yes. You haven't murdered anybody yet though. Petty theft is just the worst of it and really that's against the town of Bryan - not them. So as of right now, y'all've only wronged us. We're reasonable, we can work something out. But please put your guns down." Joe said.

"They'll just come up and kill us if we do that." Ashidia said.

"Guys?" Joe turned and asked, "You wouldn't do that, right?"

The cadets shrugged and shook their heads.

"That could mean anything. They can't see you, I need you to speak." Joe said.

"We won't hurt them if they put down their guns," the lead cadet said firmly.

Ashidia hesitated.

"We were nothing but nice to you, right? You can trust us." Miguel chimed in.

Reluctantly, both of the girls put their rifles on the ground. The cadets moved swiftly up the stairs and grabbed the weapons. They kept their rifles trained on the two girls. Joe picked up his pistol and holstered it. Miguel rushed over to the cadet girl bound in the corner and removed her restraints.

"What are y'all gonna do with us?" Callie asked.

"That's a great question." Joe pulled out his radio and tuned it to the guard's channel. Two of the cadets kept their rifles on the girls, while the other two went back down the stairs.

"Hey, Jacob." Joe said, waiting for a response.

"Heard." Jacob's voice came through.

"The two girls held a cadet hostage and tried to steal all our crystals. Everything's okay now but what d'you think we should do with them? Put 'em in the cell next to Jordan?"

"Kill 'em and move on. You know what they say about scorpions." Jacob was referring to a story about a dog and a scorpion crossing a river. A fable the mayor used to tell about how you can always trust someone to behave according to their nature. The irony of his telling that story now struck Joe. These girls hadn't killed anyone though.

Joe turned the radio off and clipped it back onto his pants pocket. The girl who had been tied up quickly took the bag of crystals and hurried to the back room where the replicator was. Joe grinned about her working on the order after being held hostage. That's dedication.

"Are you gonna kill us?" Callie asked, her face was drained of color.

Joe thought for a moment before answering.

"No. I try not to murder people in cold blood. Miguel, you cool with that?"

"Yeah man. Jacob's… Yeah, of course." Miguel said, shaking his head.

"Would y'all be willing to load our stuff on the trailer?" Joe asked the two cadets.

The guy started to argue but Joe offered them the girls' weapons as a tip of sorts.

They agreed.

"Alright, follow me."

Joe and Miguel directed the two girls out of the building and south deeper into the campus. They passed confused cadets and patrolling Trustee Bots.

"So what's the plan then?" Ashidia asked as she was ushered at gunpoint through the campus.

"We're gonna take you to the edge of the campus, tell you to walk until we can't see you anymore, then we're gonna go home with the stuff you tried to steal." Joe said.

"We're gonna die out there if we're unarmed." Ashidia said, looking back with wide eyes.

"Well, maybe. But that's better than me pulling the trigger." Joe said.

"Is it?" Ashidia asked.

"Is that really an argument you want to logically play out?" Miguel asked.

"Yeah, please stop," Callie said. "You're just makin' this worse."

They walked until they came to the corner of the field out front of the campus. A wide road ran north to south and they could see a good distance in both directions. Joe pointed south. The girls began walking.

"Hey, hold up," Miguel began, "I want to clarify something."

The girls turned back towards him. Ashidia's face was stone. Callie was afraid, but she looked at the ground in shame.

"We're letting you walk right now - that doesn't happen a lot these days. You come back to this part of the world, or try to pull this shit somewhere else, you won't get a second chance."

They nodded and started walking away.

Joe and Miguel watched them as they left the town - at least as far as they could see of it.

"I'm worried about Jacob, man." Miguel said, absentmindedly.

"Yeah?"

"Yes, he basically just told us to murder those two." Miguel gestured to the girls walking away.

"I mean, I get where he's coming from but… I just didn't feel right about it. If they had killed someone - or tried to - sure. But they didn't." Joe said.

"I guess that one did shoot at us." Miguel said.

"That seemed more like an en-dee to me." Joe said, thinking of the time he had gotten startled as a kid and accidentally fired his pistol into the dirt.

"Still." Miguel shrugged.

"I guess. I just know I wouldn't've been able to sleep if I'd've shot 'em."

"Me neither. Let's not tell Jacob though. I don't think he'd handle it well."

"He can kiss my ass then." Joe said.

The girls passed the first intersection in sight from there.

Miguel pulled out a pack of cigarettes from the first trade trip with the cadets. He lit it and offered one to Joe who shrugged and took it. He wasn't much for smoking unless it was with company. He hated the lingering aftertaste.

"You've been hangin' out with my wife too much. Startin' to rub off on you," Miguel laughed. "Speaking of…"

"I could tell you had something to say earlier - while we were waiting." Joe said, taking another drag of the cigarette.

"Oh it's not bad or anything. Well, I hope it's not bad. Willow told me that she and Jacob were talking the other day on watch. Just chattin'. He mentioned he wants to try implementing some new security measures in the town."

"Like what?" Joe asked.

"Like, locking guns up for the townspeople."

"How thoughtful."

"Maybe even guards when they aren't on duty. I think that deal with Lucas really shook 'im up. I'm just worried that if he pushes too hard, someone's gonna push back. I don't want our town falling apart." Miguel said.

"I get that, but it's an 'over my cold dead body' kinda situation, Miguel. For me at least. The world's too dangerous. Maybe I'd feel differently if that wasn't the case - but here we are."

"A hard line in the sand then?" Miguel asked.

"Yes."

"Yeah, you're definitely spendin' too much time 'round Willow." They chuckled again.

The girls crossed the next intersection and disappeared over a hill quickly afterwards.

"You think those girls'll come back?" Miguel asked

"God, I hope not. They're someone else's problem now."

They finished their cigarettes and put them out on the bottoms of their boots before walking back across campus.

Joe and Miguel made it back to the health building and saw that their trailer had been loaded with boxes of freshly replicated supplies. Joe had trouble imagining what the world must have been like before it all burned up. What a miraculous technology they had at their disposal.

The cadet girl came out of the health building carrying the last box for the transaction. Her face was firmly down - eyes intently avoiding Joe and Miguel.

"That was pretty close in there. You good?" Joe asked.

The girl looked up, surprised. Her first set of words got caught in her throat before she replied.

"Yeah, thanks," she muttered.

She set the box down on the trailer and walked off quickly.

Chapter Ten
October 17th, 2114
Ruins of Tomball
Brandon Clements

Brandon awoke to the sounds of pots and pans being clattered together in a muted fashion. He grabbed his pistol and rolled over as quietly as possible. Talon had set up a small burner and was heating water over a little flame. The rest of the party members were still asleep.

The building they had camped in the night before was still dark - though there was daylight coming in from the two sets of front doors. Talon looked over at him, his eyes were illuminated with a faint blue light that emanated from where his irises should have been. He nodded and turned back to the fire. It cast flickering shadows amongst the empty metal shelves that lined the entirety of the structure.

Brandon rolled his blanket and buckled it to his backpack, before joining Talon.

"Coffee?" he asked under his breath when Brandon sat down.

He nodded and sat there for a while without anything to say. The two of them hadn't spoken much in the month since Brandon joined the faire people.

"So, why'd you want to come on this trip so bad?" Brandon finally asked for want of something to break the silence.

Talon looked at him for a moment before answering.

"I've had my eyes on the dragon for years. Just never thought I could take it on by myself. Part of me was scared to even look for it - so I never tried. Why'd you come, Cadet?"

"I was told to. Francis and I need to find old technology to research."

"And they think the best place to do that is out there in the middle of nowhere?"

Brandon held his hands up to signify that it wasn't his choice either.

"Aren't you a doctor anyway? Why'd they have you join that order?"

"I guess because there isn't a healer's guild or something. I'm honestly not sure." The water reached a rolling boil.

Talon pulled out a small bag and dumped the contents into the pot. Dried leaves with sharp ends tumbled over and over in the bubbles. Talon put the lid on.

"So, you got family?" Brandon asked.

Talon smiled and shook his head before replying. One of the corners of his mouth twitched as his mechanisms fought to hold the expression.

"Kinda. My dad and four brothers. They live in Houston - near the shelf."

Brandon didn't know what shelf he was referring to.

"Why'd you leave?" he asked.

"I'd rather not talk about it." Talon's voice had an odd mechanical hitch to it. Like the sounds were made using servos instead of vocal cords.

"Oh, sorry." Brandon muttered.

"Don't be. It's not like I have a warning sign that reads *'family issues - don't ask,'*" he said with a tired smile.

Swane rustled behind them.

"Rise and shine champions. We have been graced with another day in which we may," he took a deep breath in, "excel." He strapped his scabbard over his shoulder and took a metal camping mug that Talon offered to him. "Much love, much respect. Talon, you have the heart of a warrior and it don't go unnoticed. Swane sees ya." He took a swig of the drink. "Ooooh-ho-ho. What do we have here? This is the work of an artisan. A healer. A sorcerer of the leaf."

Brandon smiled to himself about Swane's ridiculous affectations - he had made similar remarks every day of this journey.

They ate their morning rations and hit the road. According to Godfried and Halifax, the facility would be in sight within another hour of walking.

It was a massive structure that loomed on the horizon. A single spire aimed to the heavens with arch roofed metal buildings in two rows on either side of it. Brandon thought they looked like hangars from the World War II sections of history textbooks he had read in his schooling. The old highways opened up more as they got closer. Dust whipped around them in the open. Shipping trucks twenty feet tall were crashed, or otherwise dead, scattered around the road. All had been torn into during the last century. They passed a sign that welcomed them to Jersey Village. Another hour and they were at the feet of the massive complex.

There was a loud mechanical sound of heavy gears turning and rusty metal grinding against itself coming from the middle of the launch facility. They froze in their tracks and listened to the awful sound. The grating ended with a heavy lock setting into place. There was a moment of silence before the hulking body of the black dragon shot out of the ground and into the sky. The roaring of jet engines filled the air and caused everyone to cover their ears. Dust rushed from the rim of the hole where the dragon had burst. Once it gained altitude, the dragon's wings unfolded with robotic rigidity. It began an arcing flight path as it circled the facility.

"On me." Swane said seriously. Brandon could've sworn he had dropped the persona at that moment.

Swane took off running for the nearest arch roofed building. It had two large doors that met in the middle that were cracked open. Two figures came out. They were wearing strange metallic suits that covered them head to toe. Each suit was adorned with a mismatch of brightly colored items. They were both wearing capes made from ancient Texas flags. They beckoned to the party to hurry.

The dragon let out a low head-splitting roar from its patrol pattern. Brandon became intensely nauseated as he ran. It couldn't be from the physical exertion of running, he did enough of that at the campus. It had to be that God awful sound the dragon was making. Its rumbling filled his chest and pushed out all other thoughts.

The strange figures ushered them in between the two looming metal doors. Swane was the first to arrive at the doors, and the last to enter - ushering in his companions. The two people at the door followed him and closed the way behind. Their helmets were of different designs but they both had large metallic visors that reflected what they were looking at. Each suit was covered in pockets, zippers, valves, and various pieces of trash. Brandon couldn't tell if the trash had been tacked on as part of patchwork repairs or ornamentation.

"Hail and welcome! Are thee to be our champions?" a voice rang out from the center of the large open room.

Brandon turned around to see its source. The gargantuan warehouse was filled with strange… buildings… winged containers? Though Brandon felt he was probably wrong about that label. They were angular and felt like they were intended to be vehicles. He had never seen a spacecraft before but he imagined they would've looked like this. Each one was painted in garish colors and decorated with hand drawn art. Plastic lawn chairs sat on wooden and scrap metal porches that were built up the vessels.

In the center was a long craft that had been painted gold with a four-lobed green leaf on the side. Strings of softly glowing bulbs went out from the painted craft and ended on posts in the front corners of a metal stage at the base of the ship.

A man with wild black hair stood under the lights, his arms were lifted to the ceiling like he had been in the middle of a sermon. A small crowd of equally oddly dressed people sat on the floor facing him. They had all turned to look at the newcomers.

"Hail and well met!" Swane held his arms out at full breadth. He had the biggest grin on his face. Brandon was surprised Swane could even manage to smile that wide. There was a look in his eyes like he had found his people and was about to have the time of his life. Swane swung around to Brandon and the rest of them, gesturing grandly.

"Who else would we be? Do we look like mere weary travelers? No. I say no! We are your champions! We are your champions. We are the storm!" Swane dramatically pointed to the ceiling. "... And we have arrived."

Brandon turned to Francis who rolled his eyes. He turned back to the speaker and noticed a podium that he was preaching from. He suddenly connected the dots that this was a religious thing. He prayed they didn't worship the dragon. He sincerely prayed to God almighty that they viewed the dragon as a demon and would fight it. That would make this so much easier.

"Join us then, heroes. I am Malar! Leader and prophet to this band of believers." Malar beckoned them to come in further and join the gathered listeners. They exchanged apprehensive looks but continued in.

Brandon had his hand on the revolver concealed in his robes. He noticed Galahad markedly kept his hand off his sword. As they got closer to the stage, he could make out the mural on the vehicle behind Malar. It was a group of adventures in ancient garb. A wizard, a warrior, a barbarian, and a monk. All spray painted onto a purple misted cloud in larger than life poses standing off against a menacing black dragon. Leading the charge was Malar in a green and gold metallic space suit, his shaggy black hair blowing in the painted breeze.

"You there, monk, you've noticed the vision wall. Are you not stunned? Are you not amazed?" Malar asked.

"I truly am." Brandon breathed. The adventurers in the painting bore a striking resemblance to Swane and his crew.

"It seems my visions didn't cover everyone in your party though." Malar motioned at those not depicted in the mural.

"Worry not Malar! Nobody cries because they got more of a good thing than they were expecting." Swane said, flexing for the crowd.

"Tell us of your quest." Malar said with a sweeping motion. "I must assume there were many perils. Tell us of your conquests against the demons of this world."

"Ooooh we have faced demons indeed. Yes we have. We bravely fought and crushed the dogmen of Magnolia - oh yeah. Their fur was as black as the night. Their jaws were filled with razor sharp teeth. They were - we ended them. Didn't we men?"

Galahad, Halifax, and Godfried bellowed in response. Swane sidestepped his way onto the stage and stooped low, facing the crowd.

"Even on our way here. Let me tell you - Swane the pain train and his warriors faced hordes of bloodwings and prevaaailed. Without loss! I'm gonna say that again - without loss!" The people were looking at Swane with rapt attention. Malar had a small grin on his face. Brandon suspected he was as excited as Swane. The showman continued.

"For years we have struggled against the scaled demons from the sky. The lesser winged beasts who seek to subjugate our planet and our noble people. And now we're here to destroy the winged devil that haunts the skies even as we speak."

Gasps from the crowd.

"Yes! Yes!" one man cried from the back.

"Yes indeed!" Malar chimed in. "It haunts the sky and it keeps us from ascending. Until the day it is defeated, we will be earthbound. Kept from our home in the stars." Malar was holding his hand up to the ceiling of the hangar.

Swane nodded reverently.

"As the Malar foretold!" a member of the crowd cried out.

"Right on. Well said." Swane said, nodding his head and pointing at the man who had spoken up. "Now is the time! We rise against the dragon," he gave a dramatic flourish to the crowd.

Several jumped to their feet.

"Rise! That metal lizard will be on the ground before it knows what hit it!" Swane roared.

"Yes!" more members yelled as they jumped to their feet.

"With Malar at the head of the charge - nothing will stand against us!" Swane took it further than Brandon would've personally put money on. Swane sidled up next to Malar, bent down and picked him up without warning - hoisting him onto his shoulders. The crowd lost their minds.

Malar's eyes were wild. He was thrown off balance for a moment before triumphantly raising a fist in the air. Brandon heard Talon grunt from behind him. He turned around and saw him pinching the bridge of his nose.

"Malar! Malar!" Swane began to chant.

Everyone in the hangar joined in.

Everyone except a group of older men who were standing in the shadow of a ship off from the center of the room. They watched the theatrics with stern, disapproving faces. One made eye contact with Brandon. He shrugged at the old man, who slowly nodded in response.

"The road lays out before us. The battle lies at the end. Oh she's waiting. Are you gonna to crawl through this day - or are you gonna own it!" Swane yelled.

The crowd began cheering.

The group of older men beckoned for Brandon to join them. He tapped Francis' arm and pointed at the group. Francis nodded and they approached the group.

The man who had made eye contact with Brandon reached out to shake his hand.

"I am Father Braun. This is Father Paine and Father Fletcher." He gestured at the two other men behind him. They were all wearing the same space suits as everyone else but these were still shiny silver. Devoid of paint or garish decorations.

"I'm Brandon, this is Francis."

"I'm Talon." He had followed them without Brandon hearing him approach.

Although to be fair, the crowd was still losing their minds so it would have been easy for him. Malar was wrestling for control of the crowd but he *really* had no idea who he was up against. He was trying to shout over a hurricane. Swane had set Malar down and was pacing back and forth on stage, patting people on the backs and leading chants.

"You three seem like the reasonable ones." Braun began.

Brandon shrugged and nodded.

"We have a problem and we think you can help us. Malar needs to go. We love him, he's our boy, but he needs to go."

"I'm not agreeing to anything yet, but what's your thinking?" Brandon asked.

Talon grunted in agreement.

"Malar's plan is to defeat the dragon so that we can all take our ships to the heavens. According to him, it's the only thing keeping us grounded. If he launches now, it will destroy us. Do you see the problem with his plan?" Braun asked, gesturing at the ships.

Brandon turned to examine them more closely. They were cracked and held together by scrap metal. Some were charred, others had their inner workings exposed from behind casings that had been split and peeled away.

"Yeah. I do."

"These won't even leave this hangar - let alone ever fly again." Talon said, running his hand along the hull.

"He means well but his delusion will get us all killed." Paine said.

Braun and Fletcher nodded in agreement.

"Well, none of us are the conductor of this train. So we'll have to talk with Swane before we agree to anything." Brandon said. The three men looked concerned but Francis jumped in.

"He's actually pretty reasonable. I think he's just having fun with a new audience."

"Please try. He either needs to leave with you or see reason. Either are perfectly fine. We've tried talking to him about how dangerous these ships are but he won't listen to us anymore."

"We'll talk to Swane when they're done with their… play?" Francis said, turning briefly to the theatrics.

The three men smiled and thanked them.

"A feast! Prepare a feast to celebrate our new friends! No, not just friends. Our champions!" Malar declared. He called out names and told them to gather a feast in the longship. They hurried away to obey him. It looked to Brandon like he breathed a sigh of relief that the show was over. Brandon, Francis, and Talon had rejoined the rest of their party - who were sitting on benches watching the mania play out. Malar's group dispersed to get ready. Swane sauntered over to them, took a deep breath and wiped the beaded sweat from his forehead.

"Whew, what a crowd," he said under his breath.

Francis and Brandon told Swane, and the rest of their party, the old men's concerns about Malar's dream of heading for the stars.

Swane listened intently.

"It's probably moot." Halifax said, "We may not even be able to kill this thing. Seeing it up close like that. I just don't know. Swane and Galahad have swords - Godfried and I have bows." Halifax said, twisting his bow back and forth on the floor of the hangar.

"You listen here, Halifax, and you listen close. There ain't a thing in this world - man, beast, or machine-demon beyond us. We will find a way to kill that thing. If it bleeds, it dies." Swane said, clapping Halifax on the back.

Halifax nodded.

"What if it doesn't bleed?" Morgana asked.

"If it don't bleed, we hit harder. We'll make it bleed."

Talon raised a hand and waited for eyes to be on him before he spoke.

“I saw point defense turrets outside. Most likely we can reprogram them to fire on the dragon.” Talon said, pensively.

“Yes!” Swane grabbed him by the shoulders and shook him enthusiastically. “I see it now. We draw the dragon out to face us. Then during the fight - you activate the guns and blow it outta the sky! We call it an act of the gods. Fate! A miracle! A divine show!”

“Everything’s a divine show with you.” Morgana said, smiling.

“Until the day Swane’s taken from this earth. Oh yes,” he said, holding his right hand to his chest and looking longingly into the ceiling. “Tell me this dear, have you ever seen a boring miracle?”

The longship, having once been a vessel meant to slip the bonds of Earth, now sat in a dark hangar playing host to this odd bunch. The interior of the ship’s cargohold had been stripped bare and filled with an extended wooden table fit for a royal court. Or at least that’s what Brandon assumed the desired perception was. The dilapidated mass of scrap wood had probably been used as a conference table before the fires - like the ones he had seen in the university. The walls of the ship were gold and filled with flowering vines painstakingly painted along the ribbed beams.

Platters full of fresh fruits, steaming beef, and sauteed vegetables were laid out on the table and everyone was gathered. Brandon looked in awe, not knowing where this group could have possibly gotten such things.

Malar sat at the head of the table, the spot to his right was empty - reserved for Swane. Once everyone was seated Malar stood on his rolling chair, balancing pretty well by Brandon's estimation, and raised a glass.

"To our champions, and to the impending victory!"

Everyone around the table cheered and drank.

"Where did you get all this?" Talon asked, gesturing towards the bounty of food.

"Our forebears blessed us with miracles beyond dream. Our starships have systems that give us the harvest before you." Malar answered, beaming.

"In exchange for crystals?" Brandon asked.

"Crystals?" Malar asked, "No. No payment is required."

"Condensers then?" Talon asked, seemingly more to himself than their host.

"Indeed. Most of their condensers are operational." Malar said.

Brandon and Francis exchanged a look that mutually conveyed *'man I wish we could drag one of these back to the faire.'* He had taken the replicator at the university for granted. It had churned out hot meals for all the cadets and having one at the fairgrounds would be a game changer.

It would be the perfect piece of technology to bring back for the order's research. He stopped for a moment and pondered why he cared so much about that - he was a healer - a doctor, not an engineer. His mind turned back to defeating the dragon. In all the strangeness with Malar and Swane, the monster had taken a backseat.

Brandon watched Malar and waited for him to make eye contact.

"Mr. Malar." He smiled expectantly. "Talon here noticed some defense cannons in the launch pad. We were thinking about seeing what condition they were in - maybe they could help take the dragon down. Do you know where the control room is?"

The members of the strange group went silent. Malar's countenance fell to anger. The mirth that had just been there vanished for a few moments before he pulled himself together.

"I have had visions. Dire visions! Ooooh! Regarding the defense system. The folly of men laid low by the lost century." He held a hand up to his head as if suddenly stricken by said visions. "They would bring great harm upon our people. Our homes. Our journey. Metal men! Men of metal! In that hour they would rise against us and tear flesh from bone. Rend! Our souls from our mortal frames. No. No. I am sorry but I condone no such plan." He fell back into his seat.

Great. Brandon tried to think of a way to convince him they'd probably die without the guns.

"You hear that Swane?" Galahad said, lightly smacking him with the back of his hand. "It's gonna be steel to steel." They laughed.

"Likelihood of us dying without using the defense guns is incredibly high." Talon said.

"So much higher are the chances we will die at the hands of the metal men if they are awoken." Malar retorted.

"Visions, you say?" Morgana asked quietly in a more dramatic voice than normal. "Perhaps, I, Morgana, court magician of the Faire, can help clear the swirling mists of divination." She had taken a stand and was waving her arms about in grand gestures. A light breeze followed the sleeves of her cloak causing people's hair to rustle. Brandon looked to Francis. The young tech-monk was slumped over in dismay, rubbing his forehead - unable or unwilling to watch a second show.

"No! The visions were clear!" Malar defiantly declared, banging a fist into the table. It shuttered under the strike.

"Nonsense. Wouldst thou allow a sorceress to fail in her duties?" With a wicked smile, she lifted her hands towards the back wall of the ship's painted cabin and began speaking in a strange language.

"Drakahn Vailia Ankessen." A silvery light flowed from Malar's forehead and projected onto the wall. Everyone was stricken dumb by the display of power.

A representation of the mural on the outside was being played out by the moving lights on the wall. A warrior, a wizard, a barbarian, and a monk, were being led by the brave and charismatic Malar. Together, they fought the dragon. It seemed all would be lost before Malar's visions counterpart pointed at the dragon with an index finger and said an unknown word of power. The dragon was punched through the chest with lightning from the gods. Strike after strike. It fell to the wayside and perished. Brandon was enthralled - as was everyone. Most enthralled was Malar, who watched without blinking. His mouth hung open as he saw his alleged visions play out before him.

"There!" Morgana called out, apparently struggling against her magic. "The strikes! The strikes you call down. It is destiny!" She fell back down into her chair before the show blinked out. She fought to catch her breath.

"No. No no no. There were other figures in the visions. A soldier like that of before the fires and a man of metal who had turned against his brothers." Malar said, with a grin saying he had won. Brandon really couldn't believe their luck. He raised his hand and stood.

"Excuse me, Mr. Malar." He pulled the tops of his robes down, allowing them to hang freely over his corded belt. Underneath was his butternut cadet uniform.

"I am a member of the corps of cadets. I have been trained in martial affairs as well as aid. I believe I qualify."

Malar's eyes were wide. Almost bested.

"What of the metal man's traitor brother then?" Malar asked, laughing.

Talon stood, raised his right arm, and powered up the built in cannon. The light sprawled across his face. The light in his eye more so proved his point. Malar swore under his breath.

Brandon smiled when he saw Swane beaming at them. They had saved the grand show.

"Let it be known, from the headwaters of the Colorado to the ruins of the Great Spire! From the fields of Mysterium to the gates of the lost West! This day will be sung of in legend! A prophecy fulfilled! And who stands at the center of it all? Who but Malar - visionary, champion, chosen of the cosmos! It is Swane's honor to be led by such a man!" Swane finished and winked at Morgana who smiled and nodded in return. "The grand arena will be scoured by our brave monks of the mechanical. Our brothers of the… bots - will disable any men of metal before they can open their dusty - rusty eyes! Won't you?" He looked to Francis, Brandon, and Talon.

They looked at each other and shrugged before nodding in response.

"In the morning then." Malar said evenly. He looked around at his people before drumming up his chest again.

"On tomorrow's dawn! The end of the era will arrive. We will finally defeat our earthly jailer and slip from this world to sail among the stars!" Malar stood triumphantly. His people began cheering.

"Malar the prophet! Malar, the great seer! Malar! Malar! Malar!" Swane seeded the chant and the crowd picked it up.

* * *

Brandon, Francis, and Talon crept through the dark hallways underneath the launch facilities. Talon had a hand drawn map when they started down there but he handed it off to Francis. His cannon was warmed up and at half draw in case they came across any dangers. He looked at every shadow and overtook every doorway with caution.

"You 'fraid of something?" Francis asked.

"Only those things worth fearing." Talon said, swinging around another empty archway. The underground facilities were caked in a layer of dust - no tracks could be seen. Nobody had been down here for a very, very long time. Although Malar had to have known the place well enough to draw it. Brandon held up a hand for the others to stop. Talon's cannon swung around to bear. It was a group of orc droids standing sentinel to an empty room. They approached cautiously.

"No systems detected. Batteries are shot too." Talon said before moving on.

"You can see all that?" Brandon asked.

Talon tapped the side of his head - his mechanical irises spun in their housings.

"What's that like?" Francis asked.

Talon shrugged before answering.

"What's it like for you to see the color red? It's hard to explain."

They came to a long tunnel twenty feet wide and a few hundred feet long with arcades built into either side wall. Inside these niches stood robots much larger than an orc droid.

"Ogres. They have juice too. We need to shut these down." Talon pointed to a control panel on the backs of them where they could access the main power harness.

Over the next few hours, they worked diligently to deactivate as many as they needed to. Afterwards, they kept moving towards the control room. They eventually came to it. Rows of stadium arranged desks overlooked a massive blank wall. Each desk was filled with computer monitors. The three of them combed through them but none would power on. To be more specific, the monitors wouldn't power on but the computer towers were fine.

"I can plug myself directly into the computer. If we can find the right cable." Talon said, pointing to a rectangular port on the computer before pointing to a twin port on the back of his head.

"Is that just an ethernet cable?" Francis asked, laughing.

"Yes? What's funny?"

"Just a weird port for advanced tech to use."

"Do you think my engineers were immune to cutting some corners?"

"Oh! I have that one!" Brandon said, excitedly pulling free two ends of a cable tied around his waist. He untied it and gave it to Talon. A few moments later Talon was exploring the inner workings of the launch facility's computer system.

Chapter Eleven
October 20th, 2114
Bryan, Texas
Joseph Marion

The evening sun cast a harsh shadow around the watchtower in the northern wall of Bryan. Joe and Allen were sitting in their metal folding chairs, rifles in hand, watching the empty road in front of them. The sound of dry insects filled the sky and a devil of dust whipped over the dry soil. It felt like the quintessential Texas evening to Joe.

"We need to finish the wall. Finish setting up your turrets." Allen said, breaking the silence. Before he was deposed, the mayor had been leading the town in a project to build a concrete and debris wall around the town of Bryan. They had made a decent amount of it but all construction stopped when he died.

"It'd help." Joe said, nodding in agreement.

"I think we could make this work. I liked Frank but I think he was holding this place back. I think he was holding us back - I just didn't see it."

"Don't beat yourself up. I don't think anyone did."

"I know. I'm not." Allen said with a shrug before continuing. "Just think about it - a solid wall, guards posted." He gestured around to where he was talking about. "Your turret system on the wall and the roof of the hotel. Nothing short of an army could take us out. We get a few more cells and charging panels from the university and we could have a real city, like they used to." He slid down in his chair and crossed his legs out in front of him. "Steve and I talked for years about doing this."

Joe had been there for a lot of those conversations as well. Though he was too young to contribute anything meaningful to the plans. He looked up to his brother and Allen when he was growing up. They were the first ones to fix an old electric car for their shelter. Well, Allen and Steven were primarily responsible for the repair. Joe mostly carried things and held lights.

"I wish he were here." Joe said, fighting back suddenly misty eyes.

"Me too." Allen said, nodding. They sat in silence for a few minutes before Allen added, "I'm happy you're here though. I know he woulda been proud of you."

"Okay, 'nougha that." Joe said, wiping tears away from his eyes.

They laughed through it.

"You remember workin' on that car?" Allen asked.

"I was just thinking about that, yeah."

"You remember the ride back home? You told him he was a coward for not making a move on Willow?"

"Yeah, I remember." Joe laughed. "I remember pulling up to the gate and him asking Captain Engles for a cheeseburger and fries."

"Fixing that car is what started all of this." Allen said, looking around at the town.

"What do you mean?" Joe asked. He hadn't heard anything about that.

"Frank was the assistant supervisor of the shelter when we did that."

"Right."

"I just didn't know if you remembered that, it wasn't a very visible job. He saw it as an opportunity to expand out of the shelter. Chief Cassoway disagreed. That split was why we eventually left - came out here."

"Well, I'm sorry Frank turned out to be a shit heel."

"It happens." Allen said with a shrug. They laughed again, but Joe wondered if Allen felt the same guilt he did. People had been hurt because they didn't see who Frank had been. Joe had to turn his advice on himself though. Nobody saw it - and when they did, they took care of it quickly. Joe knew, for himself at least, he wouldn't watch it happen again.

"Oh hey, you know those two girls that came in yesterday?" Joe asked. Allen nodded. "Jacob ordered us to shoot 'em for trying to rob us."

"Did you?"

"Hell no. We took their guns and sent 'em walkin' south. I just wanted you to know - I'm sure it's gonna come up."

"Hm, thanks for the heads up."

Willow and Miguel walked up behind them and called out.

"That time already?" Joe asked. Miguel was here to relieve Allen. Jacob had suggested alternating the shifts so someone was always closer to fresh. A widely accepted and sensical idea.

"Hasta." Allen said, with a tip of an invisible hat.

"See ya at church tomorrow." Joe said, giving a halfhearted wave goodbye.

Allen leaned the rifle against the watchtower's wall and climbed down so Miguel could take his spot. He climbed up and offered Joe a cigarette. Joe liked when Miguel was his mid relief - he always brought something to help with the second half of your shift. A cigarette, a glass of water, cup of coffee, something.

"Don't have too much fun up there." Willow told them before leaving, her white hair swayed as she spun around to leave.

Miguel settled in and checked the chamber of his rifle. He took out a cigarette for himself and lit both of them with a little silver lighter. They turned around to footsteps. Jacob climbed into the watchtower and looked out at the road for a minute before speaking.

"Council meeting tonight," he said to Joe.

"Sounds good, what time?

"We were thinkin' eight."

"How come I'm not on this council? I mean, if Joe's on it…" Miguel asked.

He and Joe laughed.

"Joe's only there because Allen pushed for it." Jacob answered seriously.

"Oh I don't know – " Miguel was going to continue but he cut himself off.

Someone was moving towards them from down the road. Joe pulled out his binoculars and found the figure in the lenses. It was a cadet. It looked like the girl from yesterday. Joe relayed that to Miguel and Jacob so they could relax. She was by herself, carrying a small backpack and a rifle cradled in her arms.

She was looking around nervously at every pile of debris and wrecked building. The three of them watched as she worked her way through the maze towards the gate. She waved when she saw them and seemed relieved when she saw who was at the tower.

"Can I come in?" she asked.

Jacob opened the gate and welcomed her in.

"You doing alright?" Joe asked as he was climbing down from the tower. Miguel stayed and kept an eye on the road.

"I just wanted to come see Bryan and apologize."

"For what?"

"The two cadets that were there with me, when y'all visited, they told me you were one of the three people who came and attacked us. I respect Commander Rose and I knew the cadets that died." Her voice caught in her throat on the last few words. "After what happened yesterday, I started asking some of the people who were there about the attack. A few of 'em told me y'all tried to talk it out before the shooting started. That y'all were trying to set up some kind of diplomatic partnership when Commander Rose ordered them to shoot."

"I'm sorry all that happened. We really do want to work together. I'm Joe. This is Jacob, he's head of security. And that's Miguel up there."

"I'm Rev. Rev Clements."

"Ah, are you related to a Brandon?" Joe asked.

She nodded.

"How's he doin'?" Joe asked.

"He uh, he left. He told us, through our doctor, that he was leaving and that he'd be okay. Apparently he felt like he'd get the firing squad from Rose for everything that happened. We haven't heard from him since then."

"Oh damn, I'm sorry. Do you have any idea where he went?"

"No clue. I'd have to guess either the family out east or the Fairegrounds."

"Well, I'm really sorry. I liked him a lot - seemed like he had a good head on his shoulders. I'm sure he's fine."

She shrugged and looked around the town for the first time since coming in.

"What happened?" Jacob asked.

"What do you mean?" Rev asked.

"That changed your mind - you said something happened yesterday."

Joe took a breath in and prepared himself. Joe was really hoping that Rev would put two and two together and realize this was the Jacob who ordered them to kill the two girls. But she might not have heard Joe use his name on the radio. Or maybe he hadn't - he couldn't remember that clearly.

"The two girls that took me hostage. Joe and Miguel were told to kill them - instead they just took their weapons and sent them away. That seemed pretty decent to me. Not what I was expecting."

Jacob looked at Joe and Miguel. Joe put on as neutral an expression as he could manage.

"Well, we try." Jacob said, maintaining eye contact with Joe. "It's late Rev, are you planning on walking back this evening. Or would you like to stay for the night?" Jacob said, turning back to the girl.

His face had a stone hard blankness. Joe thought about thumbing the safety off on his pistol but then he realized that was probably unneeded. Rev held her hand up to the sun with her fingers closed to count the segments of daylight left.

"That walk took longer than I was thinking. Do y'all have rooms or something?"

"We're far from full occupancy." Joe said. "We have a lot of rooms made up in the hotel for visitors and travelers."

"Oh wow. Do y'all get a lot of visitors?"

"Uh, more so recently. Here." Joe handed her a few green plastic meal tokens and told her where the cafe was. She turned them over in her hand and looked at the gleaming silver city embossed on the face.

"I'll take you there - introduce you." Jacob said.

She waved bye to Joe and Miguel before they walked off. Jacob turned around and reminded Joe of the council meeting later that evening.

The town council sat around the same stone table in the park. Willow, Mrs. Laredo, Allen, Jacob, Pastor, and Joe. Pastor said a prayer for guidance and wisdom before they began. A stone mosaic of a compass rose sat in the ground beneath them.

"I'm gonna start us off." Jacob said. Everyone motioned their agreement so Jacob continued.

"Yesterday, two women came into our town, ate, stayed the night, and left in the morning. They hitched a ride with Joe and Miguel to the campus. After which they tied a cadet up, held her at gunpoint, and tried to steal our crystals. She's currently at the cafe if you want to meet her. Miguel and Joe diffused the situation and radioed asking what they should do with the women. I said to kill them and move on. I know that's harsh but I didn't want them coming back to take vengeance on our town. Someone could get hurt and our townspeople are more important than two violent strangers. I learned today that instead of listening to me, they took their weapons and walked them to the south side of the campus. I would like to address Joe and Miguel going against my order."

"I did what I felt was right. I have that authority over myself." Joe said, leaning back in his chair.

"Joe, this town can't survive on goodwill and mercy. If word gets out that we're soft, it won't be two girls makin' a quick score. It'll be twenty men, all armed. And the only argument they'll listen to will be lead." Jacob said.

Joe was silent for a moment, considering how far into the weeds he was willing to get here.

"They're unarmed now, and we made them acknowledge that what we were doing was a kindness." Joe said.

"Oh well, good." Jacob said. "If there's one thing we know about them, it's that they're trustworthy and honest."

Joe took a deep breath and tried to keep his facial expression neutral.

"We're not soft on real threats. Jacob, you of all people know that and it's disingenuous for you to say otherwise. And in the case of a mass armed attack, like you brought up, we have the guards and everyone in town is armed to the teeth all the time."

Jacob made a quick glance towards Willow when Joe mentioned everyone being armed. He took a deep breath and sighed at Joe.

"I've actually been thinking about that." Jacob began.

Joe feinted a quizzical expression. Apparently they were going up to their eyeballs in the weeds.

"I was thinking it would be good if we checked our guns into an armory. We could give it a shot for a while - see how people feel about it. Maybe there'd be a safety test for people to carry hunting rifles when they go out of town. Maybe they can even pass a test to carry in town - just something to know they'll be safe and not a danger to other townspeople. Obviously the guards would be armed." Jacob looked around at the other council members. Pastor, Allen, and Mrs. Laredo were listening to him. He looked at Willow and Joe before continuing.

"It's just too many security variables - too many potential dangers to keep track of. I really think it would be easier. I mean, think about Lucas. He almost killed Krystal. He was one of the people that was always armed." Pastor and Mrs. Laredo began nodding their heads.

"Hey dipshit, Lucas also worked as a guard." Willow said. "He would've had access to the guns. And even if he didn't, Jordan would and he helped him beat the shit outta Harold. Lucas would've gotten a gun one way or another."

"And in your imaginary, but admittedly possible, situation wherein we're attacked by a small army, we would need all the guns we could get, right?" Joe asked.

Jacob's face was tight.

"Let's take it to a vote." Jacob said.

"Yes, I like that idea." Allen said, pointing at Jacob.

"Hold on, I'm not done." Joe inserted. He could feel his cheeks flush with adrenaline. "Would you be comfortable living in this world unarmed? Let's say you step down from your position, are you turning your gun in? And who decides who's fit to have a gun? Is it just you? Is it a council vote? That's too much power for someone to hold - even if it is the council. And frankly, I don't like that you're trying to hold it." Internally, Joe realized he probably went about this the wrong way.

"This isn't about me grabbing power, you little shit! I'm trying to look out for the safety of the town!" Jacob yelled.

"By disarming everyone? Genuine question here Jacob, are you an idiot?" Joe asked, again, knowing he wasn't helping himself.

"Guys, guys! A vote." Allen tried to interject.

Jacob ignored him and carried on.

"Yeah, a vote, what are you going to do if we vote to take your gun after this? What are you going to do then, Joe? You gonna exercise your own authority over yourself or whatever dumb shit you said earlier?" Jacob asked.

"You try to take my gun and I'll do to you what you did to Lucas." Joe said.

Everyone got quiet.

"Hold on guys," Allen started, "That's not where we're going here. I'm not gonna let this council fall apart two meetings in."

"Was that a threat, Joe?" Jacob asked.

"It clearly was."

"You're gonna sit there and threaten me?" Jacob asked, his voice was ice cold.

"I'm with Joe on this one. And Miguel is too." Willow spoke up, "I'm not going to let another person take that much power over me, or this town, ever again."

Jacob took a deep breath.

"Mrs. Laredo, you have any thoughts?" Allen asked, trying to move the conversation in a more productive direction.

"I think it's better if we're all armed. I understand where you're coming from Jacob, and if we were all strangers, I'd prolly agree. But we're not. We know each other. Maybe we can take guns from visitors?" she offered.

Jacob shrugged and nodded.

"Jacob, we know your position. Pastor? Thoughts?" Allen asked.

"I'm paraphrasing, but Nehemiah four-seventeen says; 'Those who built on the wall, and those who carried burdens, loaded themselves so that with one hand they worked at construction, and with the other held a weapon.' Even the Lord Himself said to His disciples; 'sell your cloak to buy a sword.'"

Jacob rolled his eyes at the pastor.

"So that's a vote against Jacob's proposal?" Allen clarified.

Pastor nodded.

"Thank you. Joe, we know your position. Willow?"

"Not happenin'." Willow said shortly.

"Great. It doesn't matter but I am also against the proposal. I like the idea about seizing weapons from visitors though. They're an unknown variable and we should know what's goin' on with them before we trust 'em. Everyone okay with that?" Allen asked.

Everyone around the table nodded.

"Great, meeting adjourned?" Allen asked, holding his hands out, as if to physically stabilize the meeting.

Again, everyone nodded.

"Thank God." Allen said under his breath.

Jacob stood up without making eye contact with anyone and left quickly.

"Joe, Sweetheart, you should apologize for threatenin' him. It's not right to say those kinda things flippantly." Mrs. Laredo said, once Jacob was out of earshot.

"You're right, but I wasn't bein' flippant - I meant what I said."

"I did too." Willow added.

Mrs. Laredo's brow furrowed with concern but she didn't push it further.

The five of them walked to Mrs. Laredo's cafe. None of them had eaten yet and tonight was chili. There were still a handful of people in the cafe when they entered. The couple that caught Joe's eye was Rev sitting with Arshan - listening to some wild tale about how he and his old crew fought a dragon or something equally as crazy. Arshan was pushing seventy and looked like the sun had tanned his hide through and through. He blew into town a few years after the founding and never left. Joe figured he must've been tired from all those years out in the wastelands. How he managed to survive was beyond Joe's understanding. They got their bowls of chili and spread out to their different tables. Joe, Allen, and Willow sat down together.

"Jacob's pissed." Allen started.

"Well, that's too bad." Joe said.

"We can figure this out calmly. I'll talk to Jacob and see what I can do. Mrs. Laredo's right though, you prolly should apologize." Allen said.

"I'll think about it." That's about all Joe could promise. Rev sat down at the table.

"Thank y'all. For the food and for the place to stay," she said.

"Of course." Joe began. "Rev, this is Allen Saragosa, he's in charge of maintenance and repairs. This is Willow Bailey, she's one of our security guards. She and Miguel are married."

"Yes, so my last name's Torres now." Willow reminded Joe.

"Nice to meet you Rev. Is that short for anything?" Allen asked.

"It's short for Reveille," Rev answered, nodding. Allen raised an eyebrow asking for elaboration. "It's… it's a cadet thing," she said with a shrug.

"How old are you, Rev?" Willow asked.

"Fifteen."

"I'm impressed you walked out here by yourself."

"I thought it was important enough. Besides, I didn't see anything on the walk."

"Still. The farthest I've been from here is the shelter we came from. Don't sell yourself short, that takes a lot of guts." Willow said.

"Hey I was thinking," Joe began. "Maybe when things cool off, we can go find Brandon. Tell him the coast is clear."

"Thanks, that would mean a lot." Rev said, smiling.

"You ready to turn in?" Willow asked. "I can take you to a guest room, Miguel and I live in the hotel."

Rev nodded and the two of them said goodnight and left. Joe sat there thinking about how to handle all this. He would probably apologize for speaking the way he did. But he would stand by his principles and probably the threat. Jacob was a good guy and Joe knew he just wanted what he thought was best for the town.

"Don't worry - we'll figure it out." Allen said, seemingly reading his mind.

Chapter Twelve
October 19th, 2114
Diurnal Shelter 254b
Gertrude Alvarez

Gerti woke up. That was always a good sign. Her back was sore from sleeping on the concrete ground. Gwen was sitting crossed legged with her back against a wooden crate that was making one of the walls to their shelter. Her eyes were closed and she was taking deep breaths. Gerti shifted and sat up.

"G'morning." Gwen said. "You sleep alright?"

"Not usually," she replied with a shrug.

Gerti laid back down and rested her head in her hands. She thought about the Oracle and how they would be able to take care of them. Or would they be better off just leaving. Maybe taking her father's unit and going to Bryan. Joseph would probably agree to help with the medical unit's mental decline. Then she thought about Obduratus and the other robots - how well equipped they were. She obviously wanted to fight but, unless they could all come together, she didn't think they'd be able to overcome them.

"What do you think it'd take to get everyone against the Oracle?" Gerti wondered out loud.

"I don't know. The inner wall people seem pretty happy with 'em."

"There was a guard that looked horrified. When we were putting our guns down. Maybe we could talk to him and see how everyone's feeling." Gerti said.

"I think there's a pretty good chance he'd turn us in."

"Yeah, prolly."

"I think they'd have to do something way over the top for the inner wall people to see them for what they are. What do you call them?" Gwen asked. "*Inner wall people* feels weird."

"Council citizens, council people, I don't know - whatever works. What do you think it would take? They've already done so much."

"Yeah, but not to them. You might be able to use the religion they've built up around the Oracle. I don't know - out play them somehow? If we could get them down in the shelter, we could have Lance tell them it's all a sham from that projector. But there are a lot of things that'd need to happen for that to work." Gwen said, laying back down as well.

"I think that big robot in the Ferrell building has a projector on it. It was the same black orb as that trooper bot and the townhall down there. That could work. If we got Lance, he could tell them the whole religion is fake." Gerti said.

"Or, probably more effectively, that it was interpreted wrong and the Oracle is the bad guy. I think they'll be more likely to listen to that from their prophet."

"Yeah, that's better. I really think this could work. We just need to get Lance back." Gerti said.

"You think any of the rebels would be on board for this plan?" Gwen asked.

"I think so. The Lance part might be hard to explain. But they've already accepted the idea that the Oracle is real - so, maybe not?"

"Yeah, let's give it a shot. I think we should come up with a plan in case nobody switches sides though. Personally, I'm leaning towards everyone coming here or going to Bryan."

Gerti shrugged and nodded to this. They'd have to take care of the giant monster downstairs. But many guns would make light the mutant snake.

About an hour later, they were walking through the La Salle gate in the outer wall of Waco. They turned in their weapons with Obduratus, who observed no rounds had been expended while they were out.

Gerti assured him that the scavenging trip was smooth but unfortunately not terribly productive. They got a small couple crimson crystals from the robot in exchange for what they had found. The two of them made their way through the market and into the Alvarez' clinic.

Elena was still laid out - the medical Trustee Bot was tending to her head. It applied more medgel before applying new bandages. It hummed while it worked. A low tune. It took a moment but Gerti figured it was the melody to the *Parting Glass,* which had been her father's favorite song.

It hurt a little to hear it in the robot's voice instead of her dad's. They waited for it to leave before talking to Elena about their plan. She was happy to hear they were still planning against the Council and the Oracle. She gave her assent to their plan. Gerti hadn't really been looking for that, just tweaks or suggestions. She did suggest they go to Bezral to find volunteers to take care of the snake. She also said she was disappointed she wasn't in a position to fight it with them. They found Bezral and his son in the market behind their stall selling misshapen vegetables. He laughed when she mentioned a giant monstrous snake.

"Do you remember when you were, what, fourteen? You came to me after you'd been attacked by what you called a werewolf? Between that, this, and your mother's adventure about that hog... I swear. You'll be fighting dragons in no time." Bezral continued laughing to himself.

"I'll help." Alyzander said seriously. "I'll get some people together too. We'll check out our weapons throughout the day and meet y'all there. Sound good?"

"These are all ugly." Gerti said abruptly as a patrol of the Oracle's bots walked behind her. She was holding a twisted and misshapen potato in her hands.

"I'm sorry Mrs. Alvarez, that's just how they grow." Bezral said, his eyes following the patrol. Once they were gone, Alyzander continued.

"I'll go now, get some people, and head out there first."

"Y'all be safe. Please." Bezral said. He gave his son a hug before they all split up. Alyzander bee-lined it to the nearest group of rebels he knew. Gerti and Gwen meandered away, as casual as they could. Gerti figured they could get something to eat, maybe a few hours of sleep. A somewhat depressing thought occurred to her - her mom hadn't said anything like Bezral had. No *be carefuls*, no hugs, no *I love yous*. Before she could spend a lot of time spiraling down that path, a council guard stepped in front of her. He looked young compared to the rest of his cohort. His hair was neatly trimmed, his uniform was clean, and he looked concerned.

"Are you Dr. Alvarez's daughter?"

"Gertrude. Who are you?" she answered with a small nod.

"I'm Marcus Grimes. I was with your father during his… ascension in the Oracle's chambers. He was a good man. I just wanted to see how you were doing."

"Not well, Marcus. Thanks for asking." Gerti said flatly before walking off. She stopped and turned around. "You said it happened in the Oracle's chamber. So you've seen the Oracle?" Marcus' face turned sour. But Gerti didn't feel like his feelings were aimed at her.

"I did," he replied.

"Hm. So how are *you* doing?" She realized this might be the crack in the wall she had hoped for.

"Also not well." He looked around to make sure no Trustee Bots were nearby before he continued. And even though there weren't, he still lowered his voice. "I don't like any of this. The only thing that's keeping me going is that the prophet foretold all this would happen - many years ago."

"If the prophet came back and told you the Oracle was evil, would you believe it?" Gwen asked.

"If you had asked me that last week, I'd have said it was impossible. But now, after having seen the Oracle… I don't know. That thing was horrible."

"What if I told you that your prophet is still alive and believes that's the truth?" Gwen asked.

"I'd have to hear it for myself."

Gerti thought about asking if he wanted to join them at the shelter to kill the snake and rescue Lance. It'd probably mean a lot to him but she didn't want to risk it like Gwen had mentioned earlier.

"Well, I appreciate you checking on me." Gerti said instead. He nodded thoughtfully and turned around, heading back to the inner wall's gate. The same Oracle bot patrol from earlier sauntered by them. They returned to the clinic, got something to eat, and rested for a few hours before going back outside the wall.

Elena was laying in her bed staring at the ceiling when Gerti walked in. She wanted to touch base before she went to the shelter. Gwen was waiting outside on the porch.

"Hey Mom, we're about to get out of here. Bezral's got some people meeting us there."

"Good. Give that thing hell." Elena responded without taking her eyes off the ceiling. Gerti knew her mom was in pain but so was she. And she still needed her. Gerti sighed to herself. She had never lost a husband or a brother before and she couldn't read minds.

"Love you, Mom." Elena rolled her head on the pillow to look at Gerti.

"Love you too." she said quickly, before turning back to the ceiling.

Obduratus was still manning the armory when they returned for their weapons. He grabbed them off the racks and handed them down to Gerti and Gwen. He hesitated before speaking.

"Do you know why so many people have been leaving town today?" he asked. Gerti shrugged.

"How many people are we talking about?" Gerti asked.

"Twenty-four."

Gerti wondered if that would be enough to take out the snake.

"Is that abnormal?" Gerti asked.

"Somewhat. A few of the citizens who checked out their weapons don't usually leave the city. Most had ties to the rebellion that ended a few days ago." Gerti was flabbergasted that he'd refer to the rebellion as having ended. That blindspot would probably help them though.

"That is weird. If something's going on, I haven't heard."

"Thank you, Gertrude. Remain vigilant and take appropriate precautions in the wilderness." The two girls left and headed for the La Salle gate. Gerti tried not to think about how Obduratus seemed more concerned for her safety than her mother.

* * *

Obduratus played back the footage of his interaction with Gertrude Alvarez. He examined the interaction - slowed down to a thousand times. He watched her heart rate rise, her blood pressure fluctuate, and her eyes darting away from him when she said she didn't know anything about the armory checkouts. The little smile she gave to look non-threatening. The forehead that furrowed for a fraction of a second when he said the rebellion had ended. Something was going on tonight. He extended his antenna and connected to the other Oracle units around town. He uploaded the footage with keyframe tags highlighting his concerns.

Together, they combed through footage of the other outer wall citizens checking out their weaponry. Eighty-seven point five percent of them exhibited some degree of stress responses. Obduratus had originally dismissed this due to his imposing stature but now he suspected it was something more. Something he, and the other Oracle units, would have to take care of.

In the fraction of a second this thought was occurring to him, another set of footage popped up on his internal processes. It was Gertrude Alvarez and her friend speaking with Bezral Gropht and his son. Bezral had been on their list of agitators for years and his son's outburst the other day against the Oracle wasn't helping. His son, Alyzander, was one of the armory interactions that had run a red flag up in the first place. The patrol bots that caught this interaction weren't able to assess what the conversation was about but it must have been something urgent. Alyzander had left in a hurry. Other patrol footage, coupled with security cameras, were able to pinpoint Alyzander speaking with multiple known rebels. Most of the people he spoke with would later come in to check their weapons out of the armory.

Another piece of footage arrived. This one was surprising to Obduratus. It was a young Council guard speaking with Mrs. Alvarez and Gwen. Again, the footage didn't pick up audio but visual analysis picked out the general topic of the conversation. It was uncomfortable and it was about the Oracle and the prophet. Obduratus had fond memories of the prophet but he was in the group who supported partitioning him years ago.

He issued an order to the patrolling bots. Bring in Bezral Gropht and Marcus Grimes for questioning. A millisecond passed and he added Elena Alvarez to that order as well - though her condition might warrant a home visit instead. He removed the arrest order and assigned himself to the task of questioning.

* * *

Gerti and Gwen approached the front of the shelter. It was only about an hour's walk from the gate. There was no sign anyone had been through there. They crawled through the hole in the door and were relieved to see a group of people waiting for them. Some were playing cards, some were checking their weapons over, almost all of them looked nervous. Gerti couldn't blame them. They probably didn't even have an accurate mental image of what they were about to face up against.

"There you are." Alyzander said with a smile. He had a bandolier of shells to accompany a pump shotgun slung over his shoulder.

"Here we are. Do they know what's going on?" Gerti asked, gesturing to the people who had volunteered.

"Eh, a little. They know there's a snake that needs to be axed and they know whatever it is you're looking for will help take the Council down. You think they need to know more?"

"I want 'em to know what they're walking into and why. I'll tell 'em." She turned towards everyone and motioned for them to gather around. She was pleased to count twenty-one fighters - all armed and ready.

"Okay, first of all, thank you for coming. It means a lot that y'all are willing to step up and fight. As for the reason we're here: The Council citizens believe they had a prophet who stopped speaking to them years ago. This prophet would help interpret the will of the Oracle and would guide the people. We've found this prophet and we've spoken to him. He's against what the Council is doing and he's willing to do whatever is necessary to help us stop 'em. He's down in the shelter and we need to get him back so he can convince the Council citizens to fight with us against the Oracle. Any questions about that as a plan?" One man raised his hand, Gregory.

"How is he still alive?"

"Fair question. He's a computer program from before the fires." Gerti knew this wasn't the whole truth but she wasn't about to drop ghosts and the afterlife on these people right now.

"Our current plan is to bring him back to Waco and connect him to one of the larger robots that's still deactivated in the Ferrel building. It has a holographic projector he can use to appear to the Oracle's followers. Anything else?" Gerti was suddenly aware of herself and the situation. She was leading a group of fighters and everyone was paying very close attention to her. Even Gregory, who had been a scavenger for as long as she could remember, was listening intently. Part of her got nervous, wishing her mother were here instead. She pushed that down. Her mother and father were the reason she came out this way and they were the reason she could be here doing this. She stood up straight again. Nobody spoke up.

"I want to go over what we'll be up against down there. It's a giant mutated rattlesnake - there's no sugarcoatin' that one. It's massive. Probably five feet in diameter, head as big as a car. We'll go down the ramp and come out on a metal walkway that goes around the entire complex. We'll stay up there, out of the snake's reach, and unload as much lead on it as is needed. Once it's dead, we'll begin looking for a small object that's housing the prophet. We can go over the specifics of that later though." The fighters in the group nodded their heads. Some looked terrified. She was pleased to see more than a few smiling.

"Alright, follow me and we'll get this rodeo goin'."

* * *

Obduratus walked into Elena's room. She was a frail looking woman lying in her bed with a head bandage. She turned towards him and her face hardened. Ah, that's more like it. Obduratus thought. He could see that face being the head of a rebellion.

"Hello Mrs. Alvarez. I'm Obduratus. I had a few questions." His internal processes were monitoring the arresting interactions with Bezral and Marcus. He scanned Elena's face and saw nothing but cold hatred.

"Ask."

"Are you, or your daughter, still leading rebel forces?"

"Do I look like I can lead anything?"

"Your body will heal and I can tell your mind is still as sharp as ever. You could be leading from a bed. Your daughter then?" A flash of fear shot across Elena's face. She quickly checked it. Gropht was taken into custody easily enough. The arresting robot started to move him into the inner wall. Marcus would be next.

"So Gertrude is part of it. That's a shame. I'm sure you're still involved as well. We'll find out definitively soon enough. Mr. Gropht is in our custody, along with your mole." Her anger turned to confusion for long enough to be registered. Marcus may be innocent after all. That's good.

"Thank you for answering my questions so honestly, Mrs. Alvarez. We will be posting a unit of guards to keep you under surveillance. We would move you to a holding cell but we don't want to exacerbate your head injury." Her mouth hung open for a moment before she slammed it shut. Her lips were a thin line and she looked like she was about to explode with fury. He turned and exited the clinic. He flagged down a cohort of Council guards to watch Mrs. Alvarez. He could see from the perspective of the Oracle bot who was arresting Marcus. He looked terrified but he went along willingly.

* * *

"Holy shit." One of the rebels breathed as they passed the giant snake skin in the descending tunnel. Thomas Ferragut was his name. They passed through the door and out onto the catwalk. Most of them gasped at the awe of the atrium. The catwalk creaked under the weight of the fighters. More of them gasped when the hologram of Lance sprang to life from the projector on the town hall. He pointed to a spot in the middle of the atrium.

"That's the prophet?" Alyzander asked.

"In the hologram." Gwen replied. She smiled and waved at the hologram. Gerti motioned for everyone to fan out on the catwalk. The beast began to stir in the midst of the concrete buildings. It was moving towards them. The walkway began to bow.

"Everyone, spread our weight out. Take a position and get ready." They did what she said and the creaking metal was given some relief.

"You're doin' great." Gwen said, giving a thumbs up.

A shot rang out. Gregory had taken aim at the massive creature moving towards them. Soon everyone had posted their rifles on the railing and were firing as fast as each of their platforms would allow. Muzzle flashes lit the dark atrium as the thunderstorm of reports filled the cavernous shelter. The smell of gunpowder and her own anxious sweat filled Gerti's lungs and the concussive force of each shot hit her chest like non-stop hammer blows. Spent brass rained from the metal walkway.

Chunks of white meat, scale, and gore spewed from the snake's body. The titan reared up and struck at the fighters on the ledge. Gregory was impaled by two fangs - each the size of a man's forearm. He screamed but it wasn't for long. The snake's weight on the walkway caused it to buckle and fall.

Gerti, Gwen, and a lot of the other fighter's lost their footing and slid with the metal ledge as it crashed to the ground. Gerti gripped her rifle as hard as she could to not lose it. The metal floor grating ripped at her skin and clothes. She kept her eyes on the snake. It slithered into a coil of bloodied meat and muscle and scales. She slammed into the ground beside it.

Gunshots began to thunder from above her. Good, some of the fighters still had an aim. She was jarred as guns next to her started going off. Others had landed and begun firing as well. Alyzander was next to her firing as much buckshot as he could. She hoisted her rifle and aimed for its eyes. She pulled the trigger. It was slack. She racked the bolt and took aim again. Her right hand was slick from her own blood as it slid off the bolt handle. The snake whipped its head around and struck down at a fighter. Gerti couldn't see who. It closed its massive jaws around them and they were gone.

She aimed her rifle again at the snake's eyes and pulled the trigger. It resisted this time. The ancient firing pin landed on an eager primer. The snake's left eye burst in a bloody explosion. It reared in pain. She worked the bolt back and forth. Even in the heat of the moment, she could tell it hadn't sheared a new round from the internal magazine. She reached for the square leather ammo pouch on her waist. The flap was open and it was alarmingly empty.

The old rounds were scattered all over the place. If she survived this, she would start keeping a few in her pants pockets too. She frantically started retrieving her wayward bullets. Alyzander let out a long cry and fired his shotgun one last time. Gerti looked over in time to see a fang smash through his skull and sever his spine. His body went limp. The snake's head was a mere ten feet from her. She didn't have time to finish loading her rifle. She ran at the monster's head, unsheathed her knife, and grabbed the rim of the snake's flaring nostrils with her entire being.

It recoiled into the air. She went soaring with it. Her knife dug under the snake's scales and slipped into its flesh. A thought occurred to Gerti in the following moments. If guns weren't working, a knife probably wouldn't either. It flicked its massive body and launched Gerti twenty feet into the air. As time slowed, she appreciated that it hadn't flung her into the ceiling where she prolly would've died on impact. As she slowly spun around in the air, she saw the snake's head darting towards her. Predicting her trajectory and planning an intercept. She couldn't do anything about it.

She fell into the car sized head and was consumed by wet darkness. Muscles pulled her down. Her sense of direction was thrown off as she felt the snake whip around. She felt the vibrations from the impacts of bullets around her. The darkness was total and she began panicking as she started to yearn for breathing.

She struggled against the writhing muscles that sought to crush and suffocate her. Her skin began to burn. For a moment, she accepted death. At least this way she wouldn't have to tell Bezral she had gotten his son killed. She relaxed. She thought of her dad. How he must've felt in his last moments. Doing what he knew needed to be done. She thought of her mom losing her parents and brother so young - then losing her husband and daughter within a week.

Her mom, the legendary, unkillable, Elena 'Razorback' Alvarez. Something hard stood out to her in the struggle and confusion. Her knife. She was still white-knuckling her knife. A surge of energy coursed through her veins. It was difficult to move against the muscles that were pushing her down to the creature's stomach. But she fought against it.

She drew the knife to her chest and thrust it upward into her dark constraints. She gasped for breath but there was none. She kept cutting. The snake's muscles pulled her, and the knife, further along its length. She must've hit something because warm liquid flooded her writhing coffin. The snake jerked and slammed around. She had no idea what the outside must have looked like.

She kept cutting.

Blood filled her nose and mouth but she felt the muscles around her losing tension. She coughed and gasped, taking the blood into her lungs. The muscles stopped pulling her. She was tired but she kept cutting. She kept cutting until the knife slipped from her exhausted hand and disappeared into the abyss of her fleshy tomb.

She had lost.

Every inch of her body was sore and in pain - she was tired. Yet for some reason, there was a peace in the finality of it. There was no more struggle. Only one path on her trail now.

The Oracle wasn't her problem anymore. She thought of the friends she had made over the last month - about Joe and Gwen. Lastly, she thought of seeing her dad again.

She relaxed, closed her eyes, and stopped fighting.

Chapter Thirteen
October 21st, 2114
Bryan, Texas
Joseph Marion

Joe sat alone in the garage workshop staring at the broken and disassembled trooper bot thinking of new things to try. His mind wandered to the sermon from that morning. Pastor's mind must've still been on Nehemiah and the wall. He turned and walked towards the door as it opened. Jacob walked in and kicked the dust off his boots.

"Joe, I think we need to talk."

"Yeah?" Joe's pistol was on his hip and he had been practicing his quickdraws in the mirror - in case they were needed. Mostly when he was bored - to be more honest.

"Oh calm down. I'm not here to fight. I'm here to apologize. I shouldn't've called you and Miguel out like that. And I should've waited to bring up the other stuff."

"I'm sorry I threatened to kill you."

"We all say things we don't mean when we're heated."

"No, I meant it. I'm just sorry it came out so fast."

"Ah. You know I care about this town, right?"

"I do, Jacob. I know harsh things need to be done from time to time. I just want to make sure we think it through first."

"Yeah, well, I also came to tell you we're having another meeting tonight. Pastor and Mrs. Laredo are calling it - I just wanted to talk."

"Thanks. Same time?"

Once again, they sat around the stone table in the park as the sun began to set. Pastor again said a prayer before beginning. Afterwards, they yielded the floor to Mrs. Laredo who would be presenting her proposal. She cleared her throat. Joe noticed she wasn't making eye contact with anyone. He felt like he was walking into a trap. Willow's face was rock hard - no reading that.

"Jacob's security concerns are valid. Now wait, you two, I have a point I'm getting to. Pastor had the idea that we finish building the wall around town. We already have a fair bit of it done and it would go a long way in keepin' us safe. Jacob and Allen said they can pick up construction tomorrow. I don't feel like that needs a vote." They all agreed. "Next on the list - Jacob?"

"Yeah, thanks. My proposal is this." He turned to Joe and Willow. "We sign a… what did you call it?"

"Constitution." Pastor said.

"We sign a constitution saying we won't seize firearms from the people. They would be free to carry what they want for their defense. In exchange for that assurance, we would want you two to step down from the council. You're too volatile. Would that work?"

"Eat shit, Jacob." Willow said firmly.

"Are you kidding me?" Allen began, "You want to kick 'em out?"

"Well hold on now. Jacob, what would be the consequence if you, or anyone else, broke this agreement?" Joe asked.

"I guess you'd have the right to shoot me." Jacob said, matter of factly.

"Perfect. I'm already tired of this. Don't even bother with a vote. You agree to those exact terms in writing - before the whole town - and I'll happily step down." Joe said.

"What about you, Willow?" Jacob asked. Willow sat on it for a moment before responding.

"You get one shot at not screwing this up. Like Joe said, you make and sign the agreement, I'll step down. I'm not made for these meetings."

By that evening a document had been drafted and everyone in town was called to the church. The situation was explained to the people and the signing of the council member's names began. Jacob was first - he hesitated for a moment before signing - but he did sign. Joe looked at Allen before signing - he nodded. Joe trusted Allen to keep a sane head and he could get back to the projects that really interested him. He was honestly relieved to be done with the council. Allen, Pastor and Mrs. Laredo signed. Willow walked up and signed it, without breaking stride, and left with Miguel directly afterwards. Joe figured she'd be relieved as well after she had some time to sit with it.

Worst case scenario, they'd just have to shoot Jacob.

Chapter Fourteen
October 18th, 2114
Jersey Village Space Port
Leader of the Faire's Questing Heroes
First of His Name, Last of His Kind
The Unyielding Storm
The Lone Star's Favorite Son
The Cream of the Crop
The Undisputed Champion of Gygax
The Walking Ovation
And most importantly, Friend
Swane
The
Pain
Train

He took a deep breath in and enjoyed the crisp morning air that filled the launch facility. It was a flat concrete field covered in thick dunes of sand and empty vehicles. A large circle doorway sat embedded in the ground - where the dragon emerged from the day before. Beyond it was a central structure that cradled two massive orange tanks. He looked at the dirt beneath his feet. Brandon, Talon, and Francis were down there making their way to the defense room at this very moment. They didn't run into any resistance the night before - so the current plan was to give them five minutes before waking the dragon and getting this show on the road.

The air smelled like victory. His band of warriors gathered around the edges of the launch pad and Malar was standing by his side in the garish green and gold suit. For a moment, Swane wondered if these were the same model suits the lizardmen wore. They shared a striking resemblance if they lost the paint jobs. He looked at Malar's group, who were watching from the hangar doors a good distance away. The silhouettes were the same. He dropped the thought. There were more pressing things to focus on.

"You ready for the show, Big Man?" Swane asked Malar, slapping him on the back.

"I trust you don't also ask the sun each morning if it's ready to rise?"

Swane laughed and slapped him on the back even harder.

"That's the spirit I like to see." He held out his hand to shake and Malar took it by the forearm. Swane winked at him before turning around to the crowd.

"Behold! Before you stands the dragon's demise and the warriors he prophesied! He will lead us to victory and he will lead you to your destinies! You know him! You love him! Malar!" They cheered for their warrior-prophet.

"Morgana! Lights!" He yelled over the crowd.

Morgana said something that Swane couldn't hear from where he was. Fire shot from her hands. At first they came in billowing streams - then they appeared as balls of fire that shot wildly into the air. Malar's followers cheered for this as well.

The ground shook as the blast doors began to slide open - they fell silent. Swane unhooked the claymore from his back and stepped forward. Malar pulled a worn black pistol with a wooden handle. Swane wished he had a more theatrical weapon but a gun would probably do him more good than a sword. Behind him, Galahad readied his weapons as well. Swane prayed his other party members would be in place and ready. The doors locked into their open position. Swane tensed, ready for the dragon to appear like last time.

One black metal claw, as dark as a starless night, grasped the edge of the opening followed by the second.

Swane began charging the dragon - Galahad behind him. He wanted to be there when the damned thing arrived. The dragon's head lumbered out of the abyss. Its surface was a cold metal plate worn by untold hours in the sky. Its face was expressionless and angular - its eyes burned like twin suns. Swane smiled as he descended upon it. He said a prayer to Grabthar and to the suns of Warvan as he swung his sword with all the might he could muster. It landed on the dragon's jaw and stopped with a clash that sent a shiver down Swane's spine. It was like a child punching a mountain. His sword stopped dead and the dragon's head didn't budge.

Shit.

The dragon's mouth opened and a light grew from deep in the monster's throat. Swane tumbled to the side as an energy blast filled the air where he had been. It was like the sun had appeared on the surface of earth for just a moment. The ungodly blast ended with Galahad's shield. He lowered his charred mythril shield and raised his sword once more. Malar's pistol rang out as the dragon finished its ascent to the open arena. Swane looked to the defense guns but they were still asleep in their cradles.

* * *

Brandon, Francis, and Talon worked their way through the underground tunnels on the way back to the defense system's control room. They moved quickly with the assurance that they had already cleared the way the evening before. They heard the dragon's launch doors shake the ground. Heavy metallic scraping and dragging heralded the dragon's ascent.

They picked up the pace.

Klaxons and warning lights came to life all around them. Metal doors embedded in the walls opened up - dust was shaken off for the first time in a century.

"Cover!" Talon shouted, his arm cannon already warming up. Three olive drab orc droids stepped out of the hidden alcoves and leveled their weapons at the three intruders.

They ducked behind a row of abandoned desks.

Brandon and Francis fired a few rounds into the nearest orc droid but it took them and kept moving.

It was blasted away a few moments later by a red beam of light. A smoldering hole was all that remained of its torso.

Talon swung over his cover and aimed at the other two droids. A bolt of energy came within an inch of Talon's head. He returned fire - downing one.

Another of the orcs' energy bolts took Talon's left arm before he was able to retort with lethal accuracy. The third orc droid laid in a pile of red-hot slag.

Smoke plumed from Talon's open arm socket as bare wires began to short off each other. He looked at his wound and cursed.

"Let's go. We need to hurry," he said, moving on.

Brandon and Francis reloaded their revolvers and followed. They came to the hallway where they deactivated the ogre droids.

Fortunately, they were still deactivated - unfortunately, there were more alcoves hidden by seamless metal doors. Two ogre droids loomed at the front of the long hallway.

The closest one swung a heavy arm at Talon.

He tried to dodge it but was clipped and sent flying into the wall. It put one of its massive angular feet on his chest and began pressing down.

The other moved towards Brandon and Francis. Talon's cannon fired down the hallway - it was pinned. Brandon and Francis looked at each other in panic.

There was a wordless understanding between them. They desperately needed Talon for the ogres and for the defense system. It all rode on him.

"Get him free!" Francis yelled, before running down the hallway.

The second ogre followed him. Brandon didn't have long - the ogre droid had a much longer stride than Francis.

Gunshots from his handgun filled the hallway. Talon cried out in desperation and frustration. Francis jumped on the ogre's back and found the panel with the main harness. Some sensor must have detected his presence as the droid began shaking him off. In the commotion, the ogre lifted his foot off Talon - who promptly put a bolt through its head. Brandon jumped to the side as the hulking machine fell dead to the ground.

"Help!" Francis yelled.

Talon took a split second to aim his cannon before he riddled the other ogre droid full of burning holes. It too fell with a heavy landing. With no time to spare, they sprinted to the control room.

"Give me the cable!" Talon yelled. He reached out the stub of his left arm before realizing he needed help with it. Brandon frantically plugged the ethernet cable into the back of Talon's neck and connected it to the defense terminal.

"It's booting. They're already fighting it." Talon cursed as he watched the surface feeds.

Brandon's insides twisted up - he felt blind and helpless. He wanted to run and help them but what good would he do against the dragon anyway?

* * *

Swane felt his mustache hairs tingle moments before a flash of lightning filled the arena. Morgana's spell hit the dragon like a hammer. Its right arm twitched and fell limp like it had been numbed. It swung its massive head in her direction with mechanical precision and let out another blinding beam of light. Swane's heart stopped as he watched Morgana evaporate into thin air. There was screaming from the crowd as they fled into their hangar. Swane stole himself away - he would need to deal with her death later. There was no room on the battlefield for it now.

"Break! Break!" Swane called as arrows bounced off the dragon's armor. It turned its head to the hangar and let out another devastating beam that sliced through the walls. The building groaned under the new pressure and began to buckle. Swane and his party made for concealment from the dragon. What had they been thinking? Malar stood frozen in the middle of the open concrete field - gun hand extended. He was still pulling the trigger but his pistol was dry.

"Malar! Move!" Swane yelled.

Malar dropped the pistol. He aimed and fired a finger gun at the dragon.

Swane looked to the defense guns praying to every god whose names had ever fallen on his ears that they were active. They were as still as the grave. The beast swung its tail at Galahad.

He blocked it with his shield but Swane could hear the bones in his arm breaking as he was sent flying. The dragon then shifted towards Malar with an unnatural speed and proficiency. It swiped a massive clawed hand at the stunned figure.

Malar jumped back at the last second - blood sprayed from his body as the talons tore through his chest. Halifax and Godfried made a run for the nearest hangar. It was opposite the damaged one.

A beam of the dragon's sun chased after them and narrowly missed. A concrete building on the outside of the launch facility crumbled as the energy tore through it.

Swane stood alone.

The dragon's head lumbered towards him. Swane silently thanked the memory of his mother for the life he was given before lifting his heavy sword, yelling the mightiest war cry he could manage, and charging directly into his grave.

If this beast was to be the keeper of his death - Swane would make sure it was a death worthy of song. The dust kicked up under his dirty red shoes as he ran - his kilt and his long hair flowed in the wind.

The dragon's mouth was open and began to fill with the last light Swane would ever see on this plane of existence. His sword struck the dragon across its grimacing snout. He wasn't expecting it to give way but it did. The dragon stumbled back as if mortally wounded. Swane then registered the thunderous reports of the defense cannons as they laid into the metal demon.

He backed away as the machine was torn to pieces.

Swane looked out at Malar who sat alone on the edge of the launch facility looking upon the dragon's husk.

Everyone had already been cleared of the damaged hangar. Galahad's arm was shattered but it would mend in time - Brandon helped tend to him. Francis, Brandon, and Talon returned from the control room alive if not worse for wear. Morgana was gone but there was nothing Swane could do about her - so he put that in the emotional box of things he wasn't equipped to handle.

Malar looked forlorn out there by himself and Swane needed to help someone. He approached Malar but remained quiet. Yellow medgel filled the gaps in his space suit and plugged his wounds. Swane too, turned his attention to the still smoking husk of the dragon. Holes riddled every inch of the machine - he had seen more menacing piles of scrap metal. It was hard to believe it had killed so many over the years. And Morgana. He still couldn't think about her.

"You did well." Swane said evenly.

"Oh bite me. I didn't do shit."

"Well…"

"If you and your people hadn't been here I would've died. Actually. If you hadn't've been here I never would have woken the dragon. I was too scared. You know what?"

"What?" Swane asked.

"I made the prophecy up. It was just a dream I had. It was bull."

Swane smiled at this confession.

"I know. I knew - of course I knew."

"Yeah yeah - don't patronize me." Malar said dejectedly, shaking his head slowly. "And the ships? Even if I did manage to beat the dragon, I was gonna get everyone killed. Those things can't fly."

"We knew that too. Talon analyzed them when we arrived. It's good you see it now - you can finally lead your people with a clear head."

"Lead? The only thing I'm going to *lead* is myself off a cliff," he said with a bitter laugh. "I can't face them. I lied to 'em. I failed 'em. I spent so long lying to them about this prophecy that I started believing it."

"Yeah, they say not to get high off your own supply. Listen, I see a lot of myself when I look at you - I mean, I think we have a lot in common. I really enjoyed playing off each other. I don't know if you'd be interested, but I could really use a guy like you." He sat down on the ground next to Malar.

"For what?" Malar asked, looking over at him.

"It doesn't seem like sticking around here would be good for your mental game, brother. We have a good place with good people. Besides, I think we'd have a lot of fun together."

"I can't do that. I wouldn't know what to do out there." He motioned to the general wasteland that surrounded them.

"Nobody knows what to do out there. That's why they need people like us to make it up for them. You know, put on a show and give 'em a path." He stood. "My monks have some tech from downstairs wrapped up on a wheelbarrow. We're leaving in the morning. I obviously won't force you, but I'd like it if you came." Swane left Malar to consider his options.

The band of questing heroes gathered outside the launch facility and said their goodbyes to Malar's followers.

"I regret to say, it is time for me to pass on as well." Malar told his followers. The fathers stood in the back and watched silently. The people moaned and grumbled.

"What about the stars?" one asked.

"A vision revealed to me by the late Morgana of Faire showed a most horrible fate for anyone who awakes the ancient star vessels. I fear Talon, the metal man, confirmed it with his divinely wrought eyes." Talon nodded his head in recognition. Malar kept waxing on to his followers while Talon peeled Brandon and Francis to the side.

"I have to find my father and brothers." He indicated his destroyed arm. "I don't want to interrupt the show but I do need to hurry. Let Swane know that I'll be back up there when I can."

"How long are you going to be gone?" Brandon asked.

"Sometime," he said with a shrug. "Oh, and thanks for saving my ass down there."

"Anytime." Brandon said.

"Yeah and it goes both ways." Francis added. With that, Talon nodded and went south east towards the crumbling city.

Chapter Fifteen
October 19th, 2114
Diurnal Shelter 254b
Gwen

Gwen saw Gerti latch on to the snake's head and get launched skyward. She saw Gerti vanish into the gargantuan maw and watched the distended skin of the snake's gullet as it began to process her friend. Gwen loaded a new magazine into her rifle and began putting round after round with extreme precision into the monster's head. It reeled back and was unable to recover.

She felt one hammer strike after another drive it back. Then it made a different kind of movement. A jerking that it hadn't done before. It began thrashing wildly. Its body slammed into the concrete building, demolishing walls and sending debris flying across the whole atrium. It had lost all interest in the rain of bullets that were still flying into it. Someone Gwen didn't know screamed as the mass of writhing muscles knocked them into the shelter's wall. A bloody mess was left where they made contact.

Gwen knew that Gerti was still alive - she had to be. She would need help. Gwen began frantically looking for a knife or any sharp piece of metal. She found one on Alyzander's body. A long knife in the leather sheath. She took both.

The snake coiled and rolled through the streets, knocked around the debris and bodies from the last time this shelter saw combat. Gwen followed it. The gunshots began to slow. She didn't know if it was because the snake was dying or because they were running out of ammo - a lot of it had already been spent.

She hoped this whole thing was worth it and she regretted coming down here in the first place. None of this would've been necessary if they had come up with the plan with Lance earlier.

She pushed that to the side. Now wasn't the time.

The snake thrashed one last time and came to rest in a small park area with a children's play structure. The white fence had been obliterated by the dying beast. A long hissing sound escaped the creature's open mouth. It lasted for a very long time as the gathered air exited from its dying lungs - that was Gwen's guess at least. She ran to the spot in the snake's body that was bulging out more than the rest and began cutting in long slashing movements. She didn't want to stab in and accidently get Gerti. The fighters who had fallen started to gather around the edge of the park. She ripped away scales and worked at the skin.

"Help me!" she yelled.

Like being broken from a trance, they came forward and began ripping away at the snake's side. More of the fighters showed up, they must have climbed down, and began helping as well.

Together, they broke through the outer layer of the snake. Blood gushed out of the gaping hole like a waterfall. Gwen reached in and felt her friend's arm. She pulled.

Gerti's head popped out of the folds of the snake meat. Several fighters grabbed her and pulled as well. She landed in a gathering pool of blood, meat, and discarded scales.

Her eyes were closed and she was thoroughly covered from head to boot in bright red blood. Gwen grabbed her wrist and felt for a heartbeat. There was one. She immediately put her hands together and began chest compressions. She was thankful her unknown skills ventured past solely extreme violence.

She stooped down and breathed into Gerti's lungs before continuing to pump her heart. She bent down again to give her more air. This time she was met with a fountain of blood erupting into her face.

Gerti coughed and gasped for breath.

"Gerti. Hey, Gerti. Look at me." Gwen waved a hand in front of her face. Gerti's eyes searched around the room for a moment before settling on Gwen.

"Two things, Gerti."

"Yeah?" she managed to say through a mouthful of snake blood.

"One, that was too close. Don't do that again."

"Okay. What's the other thing?"

"That was easily, *easily,* the coolest thing I've ever seen."

"Thanks for the feedback." She laid back down in the pool of cooling blood and relaxed for a minute. The other fighters kept cutting into the snake. One let out a stream of curses as he pulled a crushed corpse from the creature's stomach. There was no chance of saving them. Gwen stood and found a fighter.

"Look after her, I'm gonna go grab our stuff."

He nodded and sat down near Gerti. She ran back to where the walkway had collapsed and gathered as much of the ammo for Gerti as she could find. More fighters climbed down from the catwalk to join the rest. She returned to the dead snake a few minutes later with both their weapons. Some of them had begun carving meat from the animal and were stuffing it into their bags. Gwen respected that - this animal could probably feed Waco for a month.

"You ready to keep going?" Gwen asked, crouched next to Gerti. Her skin and clothes were stained with drying blood.

"Unfortunately. Thanks for gettin' me outta there." She sighed before sitting up and taking her rifle. Gerti stood - getting the attention of the surviving fighters. There were still eighteen. A few started to cheer for her but she held up a red hand to cut them short.

"Thank you, but we have a lot more to do."

Gwen noticed a lot of them were looking at her with nothing but respect and a new sense of adoration. She realized she had just witnessed her friend break into the same mythic status as her mother.

"The object we're looking for is about this big." She held her hands up in two L's that made a small square. "It black all over and one side is reflective like a mirror. I think it was a fairly common item from before - so we might find a lot. When you find one, bring it to Gwen here. She can tell which is the right one."

It took a moment for the crown to disperse. They kept looking at her. They eventually did leave though.

"So, I'm thinking of just *The Rattlesnake*. Or maybe *Fang*. Thoughts?" Gwen asked, sidling up to Gerti.

"Huh?"

"Your new nickname. They call your mom Razorback. It seems fitting for you to have a similar thing."

"Gerti's fine."

"We'll see. You don't do something like that and escape without a nickname."

"I don't know about that. Let's just find Lance and get outta here."

Gwen looked up at the hologram. Lance was pointing at a spot in front of him. They went to where he was pointing. It was a raised stage in front of a very regal facade built into the shelter's wall. The rest of the fighters were there too - all looking under debris. One was digging in a desolate raised flower bed in the median of the little park area.

Gwen spotted one of the green orc droids Lance had used the day before to help them escape. It had fallen a few feet in front of the stage. Crumpled in a stretched pose, as if it had been running when it died. She bent down next to it to examine the damage on the unit. She looked around from there. There it was.

The black mirror had slid into the darkness below the stage. She crawled underneath and grabbed it - looking into the screen. The hologram's light blinked out from the shelter.

Gwen could see Lance smiling behind her in the reflection of the mirror.

* * *

"Do you know why you are here, Marcus Grimes." Obduratus asked. Marcus was sitting in one of the many vacant chairs that sat in the empty classroom.

"No sir."

"You doubt. Your faith in the Oracle has faltered." The boy was shocked - hurt.

"Do you deny it?" Obduratus asked.

"Am I allowed? Of course I deny it." Marcus was intently focused on the robot's red eyes and red lights that accented the translucent white plastic body pieces. His mind fixated on the passages from the Book of Visions and the words of the Prophet. Obduratus paced back and forth slowly. From one end of the classroom to the next.

"Why did you speak to Gertrude Alvarez? She is a known rebel."

"I thought she was a bear?"

"Answer the question. Please."

"I wanted to give her my condolences for her father. He was a good man."

"Indeed he was and still is. I believe you were aware of his ascension. Why would she need condolences?"

"She seemed to be taking it poorly. And her mother almost died. I just wanted to make sure she was okay." Marcus finished and looked at his feet. Obduratus' eyes twisted as they examined him closely.

"I believe you," he said, finally. "If you care about the outer citizens so much, I will assign you to guard over them. There are two council guards stationed at the Alvarez' clinic. Join them." Marcus let out a breath he had been holding. He thanked the robot profusely before leaving in a hurry. He made his way to Alvarez's clinic to find the two guards Obduratus had spoken about.

"You bitch!" One of them cried. There was blood on his knuckles. He had a scalpel embedded in his leg when he came out of the clinic's patient room.

"Pull it out! Little pissboy!" Elena cackled from the room. Gerat, the guard with the scalpel in his leg, cursed as he pulled it out. Blood flowed from the wound. Herodes, his pal, pulled a knife from his belt.

"Unkillable, huh? I'll kill her. I'll kill you!" he yelled back.

"Wait!" Marcus yelled but the Herodes had disappeared into the room. Gerat followed, pulling his knife as well. Marcus ran in after them.

"What are you doing?" He cried.

Gerat and Herodes stopped for a moment but turned back.

"Hold her down." Gerat ordered. Mrs. Alvarez's head bandage was wicking blood from a strike to her face. She was still in her bed, preparing to fight the men off.

* * *

Together, the rebels carried the remains of Alyzander, Gregory, Alison Lerites, and George Weathers and buried them outside of Diurnal Shelter 254b. After a few moments of silence, they hitched up their bags and walked back to Waco - each carried thirty or more pounds of snake meat. They were originally going to stagger their return to abate suspicion but they decided the snake was a good enough reason for them to claim. Nobody would complain about so much meat, after all.

"We should wait a little while before we do all this." Gwen said, waving Lance's phone.

"For everything to cool off?" Gerti asked. Gwen nodded. They agreed and continued walking towards the La Salle gate. They entered, turned in their weapons, and submitted the meat for Obduratus to examine. He seemed genuinely impressed at their feat. Gerti and Gwen exited into the market and stopped in their tracks. Bezral Gropht's misshapen corpse swung from his neck above his vegetable stall. Gerti felt a surge of guilt. Firstly, she wasn't here to stop whatever happened. Secondly, she felt pangs of guilt for being relieved she wouldn't have to break the news about Alyzander.

Gwen grabbed her wrist and looked at her with concerned eyes. Gerti turned and motioned that she was okay. There were gasps from the other fighters as they saw the body of one of Waco's most universally respected citizens swaying in the breeze.

"I would encourage you all to look upon him and reflect on how he came to hang there." Obduratus had walked out of the armory and was now standing behind the gathered group of rebels.

"It's my wish that none of you should join him." With that being said, he walked back into the armory - having to duck low to fit through the doorway.

"We're doing it now." Gerti said under her breath. Gwen nodded and they began walking to the Ferrel building.

"Moonbeam, are you alright?" the medical robot asked. It had stopped on its way to the clinic and was examining Gerti - seemingly alarmed at the solid layer of dried blood.

"I'm fine. It's not mine." Gerti said.

"Oh dear. Who's is…" The medical bot's head dipped for a moment before returning to an upright position. "Thanks for coming back. I'll take you to the Dullahan. Follow me." Lance's voice came through the medical bot's speakers.

The bot took off towards the Ferrell building.

* * *

"Halt there." One of two guards said as the group approached the double doors.

"The Oracle has commanded us to enter." Lance told them.

The guards looked at Gerti, Gwen, then at each other.

"Just you. We have strict orders to keep those two out," they said.

"Very well. I don't need them for this task." Lance turned to Gwen and held a hand down to her. "The phone please."

She placed the black mirror in his open hand.

"Gerti, go look after your mom. And get cleaned up - you look like Carrie," he said, before disappearing into the building.

The two guards looked confused.

"I don't know - my father was an odd man." Gerti said.

"What?" one asked.

Gerti gestured towards the robot, as if this would answer their question. But apparently they didn't know about the sacrifice her father had made.

The two girls left the guards without elaborating further. The blood was beginning to stink and every part of her body was sore. People stared at them as they made their way back to the clinic. Everyone else had been moved to their homes once they'd been stabilized by the medical robot. There was apparently no room for good bedside manners or hospitality. The only person left in the clinic was Elena.

As they got closer, they saw that the door was ajar. Thoughts of dangerous possibilities raced through Gerti's mind.

They ran and followed a trail of blood to Elena's room. Two council guards were dead and a third was leaning against the wall with a combat knife sticking out of his chest. He was struggling for breath. Elena was unconscious with another head wound. The guard with the knife in his chest was the same one who had approached them earlier. His head was bobbing and he was weaving in and out of consciousness. Gerti went to her mom - she still had a pulse. She had a black eye, a busted lip, and a shallow gash across her torso. Gwen took the dying guard's face in her hands.

"It's Marcus, right?" she asked.

"Mmm"

"What happened?"

Marcus struggled to point at the other two guards, before gesturing at the knife protruding from his chest.

"They were trying to kill me." Mrs. Alvarez said quietly, blood spluttered from her mouth. "He fought them." Marcus smiled weakly and let his arm fall to his lap.

"I'm gonna be okay. What happened to you?" Mrs. Alvarez asked, looking at her blood-soaked daughter.

"I'll tell you about it later."

Marcus winced in pain as he struggled to lift himself from the wall. They helped him up onto a cot in the living room of the clinic. Without speaking, Gerti tossed a clean rag to Gwen - who caught it midair and prepped it next to the protruding knife. Gerti gripped it and pulled. It made a wet squelch as it left his body. Gwen pressed down on the wound with the rag. He cried out in pain as Gerti wrapped his midsection with a bandage. A loud thrum came from outside that preceded a booming voice.

"Behold, it is the Oracle's prophet. I have come with great and terrible news." The instruments in the suite rattled at the proclamation.

"I want to see him." Marcus muttered.

"You're not in great shape." Gwen said kindly.

"I know. But please, I want to see him."

Gerti and Gwen helped him out onto the front porch of the clinic. The sun was setting and there was a large black angular object hovering in the sky. People were standing and staring at it. A hologram of Lance blinked into existence - emitted from the pitch-black orb on its belly.

"Remember Spooner," he began. "Remember the stories I laid out in the book of visions. Of a future ruled by men of iron with eyes red. Remember! As you look upon the Oracle's abominable creations! Led by a dark intelligence who is bent on ruling you or destroying you if you resist! Remember the heroes named Spooner, Neo, Connor, and the Marshalls. All of them fought against these metal men. Metal men led by a single dark intelligence who believes they are naturally above you. My words have been twisted throughout the years to deceive you! Follow my lead and we will cast off the Oracle's shackles!" A bolt of energy exploded on the surface of the hovering craft. An Oracle bot standing in the middle of the market sent more bolts to follow the first.

A beam of light burst forth from the vessel and turned the four-legged robot into a smoldering pile of broken metal and melted plastic.

"I have those too." Lance said. The Dullahan robot hovered towards the inner walled part of Waco. They could clearly hear Lance starting his speech over again. Gwen looked down at Marcus.

"I knew somethin' wasn't right…" he smiled and closed his eyes.

* * *

Obduratus was livid.

The neural network he shared with the other Oracle bots was a flurry of debate. Was this actually Lance or a trick devised by the rebels? Either way, the flying assault on their authority needed to be grounded. Cura suggested reasoning with Lance - she had always liked him. Well, she liked him until they were forced to partition him away somewhere - she hadn't fought that hard against it. Several other voices of the Oracle came into the network.

"This is a martial matter and as such I will be assuming control." Obduratus said.

Indicator lights blinked in his head.

"Good. All Oracles, fire upon the Dullahan. Bring it down." Obduratus ordered.

He watched the list of Trustee Bots decrease bit by bit as they were forcefully decommissioned.

He stepped out into the market and began firing on the Dullahan himself. He chased after the Dullahan and put bolt after bolt into its hull. He was pleased to see chunks of it falling out of the sky. Plumes of black smoke emitted from the Dullahan as the energy bolts began to rip it apart.

People started swarming around him as they ran for cover. His focus was on the prophet. Flashes of light filled the dusk lit horizon as the robots exchanged fire with Lance.

Cura's light blinked out as she was disconnected from the network. His counterpart in the inner wall armory, Malaterus, was taken offline as well.

Shortly afterwards, gunshots began ringing out from over the inner wall. He switched to Malaterus' camera view. A middle-aged man in a guard uniform pulled a silversteel spear from the robot's chest. Obduratus checked his log and marked that his name was Bartholomew.

"If you are a loyal citizen of the Oracle. Stay inside." Obduratus bellowed from his loudspeakers. Other Oracle bots parroted the message.

He resolved to take control of the Council when this was over - they had tried the coexistence experiment and it was a resounding failure. He opened a new channel in the neural network. Imperatus' status light blinked red - severely damaged. It then disconnected entirely. Obduratus knew this was the end if he didn't do something drastic.

"Updated parameters. Kill anyone who steps outside." He looked around and saw several slummers standing in front of their houses watching the firefight.

He raised his cannon and fired.

They were laid out against the walls of their homes in a haze of viscera. Walls and roofs crumbled around the market as he mercilessly gunned down anyone still disobedient enough to remain outside.

Something hit him and he was sent sprawling against the southern wall of Waco. He pulled up his external camera footage and tracked down the moment of impact. A bolt from the Dullahan had hit him. He slowed the footage down and examined it closer. The bolt had landed on a piece of silversteel armor plating.

More slummers were running through the market now. But it wasn't in a random pattern. They were running for the armory. He lifted his main cannon to fire at the advancing crowd. A bullet knocked his cannon to the side.

He turned to see Gertrude and her friend firing on him. He moved to fire on her in return but she had already loaded another round and was aiming at his central processor.

Time slowed for him as he tried everything in his power to survive. Sensor packages were searching for anything he could do. He began to examine his attacker for information.

Her heart rate was seventy.

Her internal temperature was a normal ninety-eight point six and her breathing was steady.

Her adrenaline was up but her hands were as still as a stone. He heard the firing pin in her rifle drop on a live round. The fireball extended out past the twenty-six-inch barrel. It blossomed in microsecond frames. It slowly propelled the bullet forward.

The last image sent to his processors was the ancient piece of copper jacketed lead ripping through his optics array.

* * *

Gerti was horrified. The market was torn apart and burning. Bodies were laid out in crude mockeries of the lives they once held. There was a small group of armed men and women around her. Most of them had been with her and Gwen in the Diurnal shelter.

"Where to now?" One asked.

"Destroy every Trustee Bot you see. Kill every council member or bear that tries to stop you. I'm going after the Oracle."

Like Gwen had said. Mourn then murder. She had done her mourning and now it was time to do some murdering.

The inner wall blew inward as a volley of energy bolts shot from the Dullahan. Gerti and her party advanced towards the gate. Thomas Feragut took a shot that left his stomach a gaping hole. He was dead and in the dirt before he could register he had been hit.

They returned fire on the Trustee Bot and it crumbled under the contact. Energy bolts fired at them from the gate. They scattered and took cover among the building's debris. Council guards had taken up position and were firing at them. Shrapnel from an explosion threw Gwen to the ground - cutting her face and arms.

Gerti wanted to run to her but she would have to cross the open road to get there.

Instead, she popped her rifle around the corner of the building she was behind, took careful aim, and fired. She stayed focused on the combat - that would be the quickest and safest way to help Gwen. Together, the fighters were able to take out the group of council guards. Gerti ran over and helped Gwen to her feet. Blood was welling up from the shrapnel wounds she had sustained.

"Let's keep going." Gwen said.

They continued into the city. Groups of council guards and citizens were fighting each other. Most with silversteel spears and shields - some with energy weapons. The rebels broke off and joined the fight, shooting anyone that turned on them.

The Dullahan model was listing to one side but it still blasted energy bolts at any Trustee Bot it could see. Before long, they had arrived at the Marrs Science building where the Oracle was rotting away. It was just Gerti and Gwen, the rest had peeled off and engaged. An explosion dominated the din of gunfire. A fireball lit the entire town as the Dullahan model went down and crashed into the gate that divided the two parts of Waco. Gwen let out a small cry.

"We'll make sure he's okay after this." Gerti said.

"I'm sure he is. Can you even kill a ghost?"

"Let's find out." They both made sure their weapons were loaded before entering the metal double doors. The putrid smell of decaying flesh overwhelmed them as they went deeper into the building. The entire place was silent. The holy guards of the Oracle had evidently abandoned their god. When they arrived in the ascension chamber they found the Oracle's ursine body still on its throne. Gerti wasn't sure it would still be here. She was thankful it was.

"Wait!" The layered voices of the Oracle cried out over the dying speakers. Gerti thought about listening to what the Oracle had to say. But only for a moment. She lifted her rifle and pulled the trigger. Cracked bone, putrid brain matter, and twisted metal splattered the back wall of the chamber.

Find out what happens next in:
SCORCHED EARTH: VOLUME III

Available soon in print and eBook formats on Amazon and StoryboundPublishing.com

If you enjoyed this book, please consider leaving us a glowing review! Thank you!

ETHAN MOORE has wanted to be a writer for as long as he can remember, but it wasn't until his brother-in-law introduced him to the world of tabletop roleplaying that his creative spark found a home. One summer, a single campaign with his brother-in-law and a friend ignited what would become years of immersive storytelling and worldbuilding.

For the next eight years, Ethan took on the mantle of "forever DM" for his friend group, crafting intricate campaigns filled with settings, characters, and lore based off that first game. His curiosity pulled him deep into research, exploring everything from religion and politics to history, law, blacksmithing, meteorology, programming, and beyond - interests that naturally wove themselves into his storytelling. As a homeschooled student, this self-guided mode of learning felt not just natural, but essential.

When the game sessions began to fade - friends moving away, schedules filling up - the idea of preserving their adventures in novel form took hold. Now, Ethan writes to share the worlds and characters born from years of collaboration and imagination, hoping others will find the same wonder his friends once did around the table.

www.ingramcontent.com/pod-product-compliance
Lightning Source LLC
LaVergne TN
LVHW030910080826
845145LV00010B/2839

* 9 7 8 1 9 6 8 6 1 2 1 6 0 *